BUSINESS-DEAL BRIDE

DANI COLLINS

PRESENTS

If you purchased this book without a cover you should be aware that this book is stolen property. It was reported as "unsold and destroyed" to the publisher, and neither the author nor the publisher has received any payment for this "stripped book."

Recycling programs for this product may not exist in your area.

ISBN-13: 978-1-335-21359-4

Business-Deal Bride

Copyright © 2026 by Dani Collins

All rights reserved. No part of this book may be used or reproduced in any manner whatsoever without written permission.

Without limiting the exclusive rights of any author, contributor or the publisher of this publication, any unauthorized use of this publication to train generative artificial intelligence (AI) technologies is expressly prohibited. Harlequin also exercises their rights under Article 4(3) of the Digital Single Market Directive 2019/790 and expressly reserves this publication from the text and data mining exception.

This is a work of fiction. Names, characters, places and incidents are either the product of the author's imagination or are used fictitiously. Any resemblance to actual persons, living or dead, businesses, companies, events or locales is entirely coincidental.

For questions and comments about the quality of this book, please contact us at CustomerService@Harlequin.com.

TM and ® are trademarks of Harlequin Enterprises ULC.

 Harlequin Enterprises ULC
22 Adelaide St. West, 41st Floor
Toronto, Ontario M5H 4E3, Canada
www.Harlequin.com

HarperCollins Publishers
Macken House, 39/40 Mayor Street Upper,
Dublin 1, D01 C9W8, Ireland
www.HarperCollins.com

Printed in Lithuania

Canadian **Dani Collins** knew in high school that she wanted to write romance for a living. Twenty-five years later, after marrying her high school sweetheart, having two kids with him, working at several generic office jobs and submitting countless manuscripts, she got The Call. Her first Harlequin novel won the Reviewers' Choice Award for Best First in Series from *RT Book Reviews*. She now works in her own office, writing romance.

Books by Dani Collins

Harlequin Presents

Awakened on Her Royal Wedding Night
Marrying the Enemy
Husband for the Holidays
His Highness's Hidden Heir
Maid to Marry
Hidden Heir, Italian Wife
The Greek's Wife Returns
Boss's Christmas Baby Acquisition

Bound by a Surrogate Baby

The Baby His Secretary Carries
The Secret of Their Billion-Dollar Baby

Diamonds of the Rich and Famous

Her Billion-Dollar Bump

Visit the Author Profile page
at Harlequin.com for more titles.

To my amazing fellow authors writing for Presents, past and present. Writing can be a lonely occupation, but this supportive bunch is always ready to celebrate milestones and commiserate over manuscripts that won't write themselves.
I wouldn't have this career if these fabulous authors hadn't written all these fabulous books that have entertained and inspired me for decades.
I love and admire every one of you.

CHAPTER ONE

AXEL SEVERIN READ through the marriage contract again. He had only one question for the man who had been his employer and mentor: Why was the name of his prospective bride not spelled out on these pages?

He didn't ask, though. He already knew the answer.

Otto Braun had no love for his daughter. She was "the biological issue of Otto Braun." Otto took every opportunity to dismiss Mira. It was among the many reasons Axel had agreed to this arrangement—to compensate Mira for the glaring injustice of her father's disregard.

Axel wasn't a particularly compassionate man, but he did know right from wrong, and the way Otto treated Mira was wrong.

"Problem?" Otto asked gruffly from behind his marble-topped desk. He was a barrel-chested man well into his sixties. He wore his customary charcoal suit with a dark blue tie. His hair and beard were white and neatly trimmed. His eyes held the gleam that warned he was at his most cagey.

"Simply doing my due diligence," Axel replied, even as he braced like a spider perceiving vibrations in the web.

The contract stated clearly that, on the date of their

marriage, Otto would allow Axel to assume full control of the global engineering firm. That meant he would no longer be plagued with Otto's last-minute interference. Then, after a full year of marriage, Otto would sign over his shares in Vorstoben to Axel and his wife.

It was exactly what Otto had promised Axel two years ago, when Axel had told him he was leaving to start his own firm.

Stay, Otto had urged. *I'll promote you to CEO. Marry my daughter, and I'll gift the company to the two of you.*

Axel had already been chafing under a decade of Otto's dictates. He had caught Otto's notice when he'd been a hardworking junior engineer of twenty-two and had been climbing the corporate ladder ever since. In the beginning, earning money had been Axel's sole aspiration. Once he had his mother squared away, however, and built enough of an investment portfolio to ensure he would never fall back into the nothing he'd come from, he'd been ready to do bigger things. To be his own boss.

What if Mira doesn't want to marry me? Axel had asked Otto.

I'll never leave the company to her, was Otto's dismissive reply. *I wish I had a son. Marry my daughter, and I'll have one.*

The offer was too good to pass up. Sitting behind the CEO desk for the last two years, Axel's ability to curb Otto's worst impulses had resulted in steady expansion and record profits. He felt very proprietary toward Vorstoben these days. He ran it well and wanted it.

He glanced at Mira. She was a polished brunette in a dark skirt suit, hair in a stylish chignon, face drawn with strain. Axel had known her as long as he'd known Otto. He considered Mira a friend to the extent that either of them was capable of a close relationship. In reality, his predominant feeling toward her was pity. She had joined the firm after finishing her business degree three years ago. Since then, she had worked tirelessly to earn her father's good opinion—while Otto took every opportunity to erode her confidence. He was cold and critical and dismissive for no reason that Axel could discern.

She was Otto's only child. She ought to inherit the company and everything Otto possessed, especially when she had done her best to contribute to its success. Otto had deliberately held her back, though, refusing to promote her beyond a midlevel accounting position. She yearned to be taken seriously. To be *noticed*.

So, in an attempt to appease Otto and have a real chance at rising in the ranks here, Mira had agreed to Axel's proposal.

Every time they had tried to set a date for the wedding, however, Otto had pushed them off. It had become enough of a frustration that Axel had issued an ultimatum last month. Otto had to make good on his promise or he was leaving.

Finally, the contract was in his hand. No more delays. Once they signed it, they could marry. Otto would retire and, in a year, Axel and Mira would jointly take possession of Otto's shares, giving Axel the de facto ownership he'd been promised.

Mira's jaw was set with hurt that her father hadn't had the decency to put her name on the document beyond her signature line at the bottom, under a statement about her being of sound mind and agreeing to the conditions set forth herein, but she scrawled her name upon it.

Axel took the pen and rasped his name with a few hard strokes of black ink. He handed the pen to Otto.

Otto signed. Otto's assistant witnessed and left the room.

Otto handed the contract to his lawyer, Umberto, a sixty-ish man who had a weariness in his expression that Axel knew had been stamped there by decades of working with the intractable Otto. Axel often thought he would look like that himself if he didn't step onto his own path soon.

Which he was doing today. *Finally*. His inner tension eased.

"Give him the other," Otto said.

Axel's shoulders snapped back to rigidity.

Umberto didn't meet Axel's gaze as he placed the signed contract into his briefcase and offered a fresh envelope.

An acidic pang of premonition entered Axel's gut. It was a sensation from his childhood, the one he had experienced every time the class bully noticed the new kid in school. Or his mother's drug dealer had shaken him down for money she owed. Or the landlord had turned them out because he didn't like finding his mother unconscious in the stairwell.

That sensation of being powerless—helpless—was suffocating. Axel had grown out of being a victim, though. He was too self-sufficient. Too *smart*. Wasn't he?

His hand turned cold as he took the envelope and

broke the seal. He glanced at Mira. She bit her lip, watchful, expression mirroring his sense of dread.

Axel held the pages so she could read with him.

The first was a paternity report from twenty years ago. It stated Mira was *not* Otto's daughter.

Mira's shocked gasp cut through the thick silence. She grasped at her throat as though the noise had caused a physical tear there. She shot a glare of stunned hurt at Otto. "This is why you've always been such a bastard to me?" she asked on a gust of disbelief. Then she turned on Axel to accuse, "You knew?"

"No." He felt concussed by this. He was dazed, unable to work out what it meant beyond a realization that Otto had tricked him. If Mira wasn't Otto's daughter, the contract they'd signed meant nothing. This entire engagement had been a ploy to keep him here so he wouldn't strike out on his own.

A ball of fury began to condense in his gut.

"Read the rest," Otto commanded.

Axel turned to the next page. It was a notarized letter to Otto from a woman named Lorena Fontaine, dated three years ago.

As I face the end of my life, I find myself regretting that I never told you I gave birth to your child...

"Oh my God." Mira recoiled.

Mira's mother had been expecting Mira at the time, the letter continued. Lorena knew Otto wouldn't leave his wife. She provided the name of the agency in America where Otto's daughter had been relinquished for adoption.

"How could you *do* this?" Mira's fingertips lined up against her quivering bottom lip.

Marry my daughter...

Axel was far more practiced at stuffing his reactions deep into a cavern within himself. While Mira was exchanging heated words with Otto, asking about who might have fathered her, Axel was slipping into survival mode. His agile mind quickly filtered through his choices.

He could walk out. This bait-and-switch of Otto's was unforgivable. He'd kept Axel here under false pretenses, setting Axel back on his goal to form his own company. It would be thriving by now if not for this subterfuge. It would serve Otto right if Axel left Vorstoben in the lurch. The conglomerate would falter under the older man's erratic command. Axel could pick over its bones soon enough.

Or he could remain here as CEO under Otto. It was not an attractive option, but Otto would die eventually and the board would likely keep Axel on. At some future date, Axel would gain full control of the company, if not the ownership of it. *If* he wanted to be patient a little longer.

He didn't.

"Umberto believes he's found her." Otto's deep voice cut into Axel's churning thoughts. "I have instructed him to reach out and request she take a paternity test. Once we have a positive result, he'll ask her to come meet me. If she's willing to marry you, then I will make her my heir and honor that contract." Otto nodded at the briefcase, looking smug.

Or I could do that, Axel mentally acknowledged, even as he saw how Otto was trying to keep him on a string while bringing a third puppet into this farce. Otto wanted to hold his biological daughter like a carrot before Axel and keep him dancing.

"You bastard." Mira was trembling with fury. "Why did you even keep me around? Why did you stay married to Mama after you learned that?" She flung a hand at the pages Axel still held. "Why have you let us believe for *two years* that you wanted him to marry *me*?"

"To keep me here," Axel said through his teeth, so filled with disgust he could hardly contain it.

"I didn't care for the scandal. Until I learned I had a *real* daughter—" Otto's lip curled disdainfully "—I had to carry on with the charade that you were mine."

"Liar," Mira choked. "You wanted access to Mama's money. You knew she would have taken all her assets and more besides if you divorced her. I *will* take them," she warned, sending a vindictive look between Otto and Axel. "That will sting, won't it?"

It would. Vorstoben had leveraged against properties that belonged to Mira through her mother. She had allowed those arrangements because she had been desperate for Otto's good favor.

It was yet another nefarious motive for this false engagement Otto had engineered.

Axel had believed himself inoculated against being taken advantage of. He wasn't naive, but he hadn't seen that Otto was deceiving him this entire time. It made him livid, but he didn't allow any of that volatile emotion to bleed into his tone or expression.

"Is that contract worth the paper it's printed on?" he asked Umberto. "After such blatant misrepresentation?"

Umberto's wince claimed he was only following orders.

"I am the majority shareholder. I can dispense those shares as I see fit," Otto asserted, telling Mira, "There's a settlement offer in there if you keep this out of the press. But I can bequeath Vorstoben to my *biological* daughter if I want to. *If* you marry her," he added, turning the cunning gleam in his eye onto Axel.

He really thought he had Axel over a barrel.

"You've finally given me something I wanted. *Freedom*," Mira bit out, no longer the meek, biddable daughter Otto had conditioned her into. "Prepare to be made sorry, old man."

"Mira," Axel said as she headed to the door.

"No, Axel." She flung around to face him. "Do whatever you have to. Marry his *real* daughter if you want to. I don't blame you for trying to get what he promised, but take a lesson from this backstabbing. He'll find another way to undercut you. He always does." Her eyes were glistening as she shot Otto a final look, but they weren't tears of hurt or sadness. It was the glow of vengeance.

A similar flame had been lit inside Axel, an incendiary refusal to lose again. He *would* get what had been promised to him.

He folded the envelope Umberto had given him and tucked it inside his suit jacket. If Umberto could find this secret baby of Otto's, so could he.

CHAPTER TWO

Joy Youngston was midway through a stag spin on the pole when she glimpsed *him* entering the club.

Her grip almost slipped. She wasn't sure why. It wasn't as though she recognized him. She only clocked him as not someone she'd seen before. Someone she *would* remember because he brought such an aura of wealth and sophistication in with him. Power. Not only was he not a regular to this club, he didn't belong on this side of the city. Not in that suit. It must have been made for him because it moved as though it was part of him, accentuating the line of his wide shoulders and the length of his legs.

She mindlessly continued her routine, swinging around and kicking out her legs in a provocative eye-opener, then hooking the pole behind her knee so she could catch the spiked heel of her shoe and lean back in a rainbow.

As she held the position, she watched his upside-down image walk unhesitatingly toward her. His movements were as fluid as an athlete's, his bearing tall and commanding. There was a watchfulness to him. Not fearful. Aware. He recognized the dangers in a club like this, especially to a man who looked like he carried abundant cash and a nice watch, but he was blade-sharp and ready to respond to any sort of trouble.

She contorted into a back arch, then grasped the pole and brought her legs down, one–two, before sinking into splits against the stage.

Other men watched the titillating movement of her breasts or tried to catch a wardrobe malfunction in her string bikini. This one kept his attention on her face.

She couldn't help staring back. He had a square, clean-shaven jaw and straight, dark eyebrows to match his straight, closely shorn dark hair. He was more compelling than conventionally attractive. Roughly hewn and uncompromising. Beautiful in the way of wrathful storms.

Disapproving?

A savage pain hit her breastbone. *Go to hell*, she thought darkly, trying to retreat into her bubble of self-containment, but he had pierced her shell from the second he walked in. She couldn't look through him the way she usually could. Couldn't look away, either. He was too magnetic, pulling her gaze against her will.

Anxious electricity zipped in opposing currents under her skin, setting all of her buzzing. She tried to hide his effect on her as she swung her front leg around to meet the back and pushed against the stage, first a cobra, then she hinged her knees and lifted her butt high while her chest pressed low to the floor in a speedbump.

His piercing gaze didn't slide to the undulation of her body. He didn't look at her thighs with the garters she wore around the tops of them, or the tulle skirt that was more of a ruffle since it started at her tailbone and ended above her mostly bare cheeks. He didn't acknowledge the girls on the other two poles at all.

Joy did these moves for hours every night. It was pure

muscle memory and didn't usually cause her pulse to pick up or her breath to labor.

Tonight, her bones felt like melted crayons. Her limbs twitched with conflicting signals. She grew breathless and hot. Wired.

Because the way he stared into her soul thrust alarm into her belly.

And spiraled erotic shivers into her blood.

His lips moved. He didn't try to compete with the music, but she read her name as he shaped it. Not her stage name. Her legal name, Joy Youngston. He jerked his head in a signal to leave the pole and talk to him.

Her heart dipped in shock. She had the sudden fear she was about to be arrested. Exotic dancing was strictly regulated in Illinois, but she had her paperwork in order. She abided by all the rules—no touching chief among them.

Still on her hands and knees, she held his gaze as she slid her toe back along the floor, extending one leg. She reached up and back to find the pole, readying to mount it again, letting him know she didn't take orders from strangers.

He drew a money clip from his jacket pocket and pulled a hundred-dollar bill from it.

She stayed exactly as she was. The position opened the front of her body for his perusal. Still his gaze stayed locked with hers in a battle of wills that felt dangerous and exciting and terrifying.

He jerked his head again, but she wasn't giving up her spot on the stage for anything less than what she normally took home from a six-hour shift.

She lifted her chin, urging more from the clip.

He thumbed a second and a third bill, then held them out to her.

She took the money and tucked the notes under the strings at her hip, then rolled to take a low grasp on the pole with both hands. In a blatantly sexual move, she planted her feet and slowly lifted her hips, straightening her legs so she was bent forward, facing him. She held the pose with her shoes spaced wide while she exaggerated the dip in her lower back, affording him a good view of her breasts as they swayed inside the tiny cups of her black bra.

It was a little treat for his generosity and a show of insolence on her part. She would cooperate, but in her own time.

Slowly, she climbed her hands up the pole until she was standing straight. She pointed to the batwing doors that wore an Employees Only sign.

"Wait there," she mouthed before she walked backstage into the dressing room. Her knees were weak, and her pulse knocked around her rib cage like a pinball.

"What's wrong?" The girl on break was touching up her toenail polish.

"I have to meet someone." Joy pulled on a cheap blue bathrobe with yellow ducks, having learned that anything nicer than this grew legs and walked away. "You can take my spot."

"Yeah? Thanks. I need the money." The young woman hopped to her feet.

Don't we all, Joy thought as she filled a clean glass from the water cooler and gulped it down.

Was that guy from the government? The military? Her brother was serving overseas. Her sister-in-law was pregnant in California. She would be informed if anything had happened to David. What about their father? Paul Youngston was on medication for Parkinson's, and Joy had made sure he had taken it before she left home this afternoon. Their neighbor, a retired nurse, came by in the evenings to check on him and help him into bed. If there was a problem, she knew to reach Joy here at the club or when to call an ambulance.

"Joy Youngston?" The voice was like black coffee, dark and bitter.

She spun around to face him. "You're not supposed to be back here."

The lights were brighter in the changing room, glaring an unflattering yellow. She could see his suit was navy, not charcoal, and held a fine pinstripe. His tie was silver blue, like his eyes. He would be able to see her makeup was applied heavily with thick eyeliner and lips that were artfully painted to appear plumper than they really were.

"Who are you?" She lifted her brows in the haughty way she'd learned to face down all forms of male attention, whether shy or friendly or aggressive.

His stare was…impossible to read. Not lecherous, but sexual energy crackled on the air. She normally felt she had the upper hand when she knew she was desired, but she realized she had never been attracted to the men who came onto her.

This stranger had reversed that on her. She found him compelling but also intimidating. He was delving into her gaze as though looking for something. As though deciding something. It set her back on her spiked heels.

Want me. She hated that deep yearning, but she had

come to accept it was written into her DNA. Or had been stamped there with the seal on her adoption certificate.

"Axel Severin." He had a slight accent, one that rounded the *A* to *ah* and threw the *X* into the back of his throat. "You've been ignoring my messages."

Her heart swerved. She belted her robe more tightly.

"This is about my birth father?" Her ears rang with alarm. She had started receiving weird messages from Germany a week ago. "It's a nice variation on the foreign prince scam, but..." She managed to sound pithy as she cocked a negligent hip and shrugged, even though she was unsettled that this had escalated into a confrontation at her workplace. "Dancing on a pole does not make me stupid. Kindly take me off your list of potential marks and never contact me again. Willis!"

She hoped the bouncer had noticed him come back here and stationed himself nearby in case there was trouble.

Willis poked his head in.

"Can you show him the exit, please?"

Willis gave Axel an up-down glance and set his jaw, expecting resistance. Axel was close to Willis's six-five, but Willis was built like a bulldozer and removed angry drunks on the regular.

Axel was neither angry nor drunk. He was also formidable enough to halt Willis with a casually raised hand. "You can spare me ten minutes for a conversation," he said to Joy.

The messages had been unsettling her for days. She might have taken them more seriously if she'd actually been looking for her birth father—or if these messages hadn't withheld her birth father's name because "a great deal of money" was involved.

"If it seems too good to be true, it is." She'd learned that when her college boyfriend had talked her into using her own college fund to pay his tuition, claiming he would support her once he completed his degree and was established as an orthodontist.

"I didn't say there weren't strings," Axel said with a derisive twist of his lips. "Let me tell you what they are."

She blamed herself for this. She was fairly open about the fact that she was adopted. She had even let a friend interview her about it for a lifestyle blog when she'd still been living with Todd. She had specifically mentioned how frustrated she was that she didn't have any information on her birth father. It would be very easy for someone to read that post and decide she was a ripe target for a scam like this.

"Who are you?" she demanded. "A lawyer or something?"

"Or something."

Okay, Captain Cryptic.

"Look, my time isn't free." She inspected the miniature kiss prints on her black nail polish. "If you want to talk to me, we can go into the Champagne Room. It's a thousand dollars for twenty minutes." It was actually two hundred for thirty, but she was trying to scare him off.

He offered Willis a black credit card. "Give us an hour."

CHAPTER THREE

The bouncer started to lead Axel out of the changing room, but Joy hung back to flick through a rack of costumes.

"What are you doing?" he asked her.

"Changing." Her chin came up so she could look down her nose at him. "What would you like? Schoolgirl? Librarian? Bondage? Cheetah?"

"That." He nodded at her robe, trying not to think of the lush curves barely contained by her provocative black bra and butt-floss bottoms. The way she had stared at him while writhing had caused exactly the reaction intended, which was irritating in the extreme. He needed cold clarity, not dull-witted lust. Not a hot weight throbbing behind his fly, urging him to rearrange his priorities.

How was he supposed to erase from his mind that image of amber-honey limbs moving with superb grace, though? Or platinum-streaked hair falling around her shoulders and across her cheek, begging his fingers to brush it from her eyes and tuck it behind her ear? A mutinous, pouted mouth that—

Stop.

What the hell was she even doing here? His research

had told him she was studying to be a nurse, not working as an exotic dancer.

The woman he was contractually obligated to marry was a stripper.

Axel strove to be a modern man who didn't judge other's choices. He'd been in the position of having few choices himself. He knew you had to make the best of what little you had. God knew, there'd been a time when he would have thought being able to afford a private room in an adult-entertainment establishment was the height of luxury—not that he had ever thrown his money away in places like this.

He curled his lip as he entered the round room with its cushioned bench and pole in the middle. A funk of sour beer and sweat permeated the air.

He had scratched tooth and nail to get out of traps like this and resented the hell out of Otto—and this woman—for dragging him back into this world, even for a minute. If he wasn't so furious at Otto, so determined to win this hand and the pot, he would have walked out and never looked back.

Even as he thought that, however, his gaze snagged on a muscled calf and a narrow foot in a black stiletto. The turn of her ankle kicked fresh lust into his groin.

"I'll be back with the champagne," the bouncer said.

"Don't bother." Axel had had champagne. They didn't serve it here.

The bouncer left, enclosing them in silence.

"I don't have my phone for the music." Joy adjusted the knob on the wall near the door, filling the room with the relentless rhythm playing in the front of the club.

She was trying to seize the upper hand. He recognized the tactic because he did it himself with a shake of his head. She lowered the volume to silence again.

"Are they recording us?" He glanced at the dark bubble protecting a camera lens above the closed door.

"They watch to be sure there's no touching. Martini could lose his license."

Which probably didn't stop the behavior from being tolerated if the dancer was willing and the customer was known to be discreet.

How would she react if *he* touched her?

He yanked his mind from going down that path.

"Why do you work here?" he asked in a voice that sat like grit in his throat.

"A deep need to express myself through the art of exotic movement." She set the inside of one spiked heel against the base of the pole, picked up her inner leg, and grasped the pole as she leaned out, taking a slow spin around it.

Her long hair fell in a curtain that brushed his sleeve as she went by. She batted purple lashes at him and offered a buttery smile.

"You need the money," he surmised.

She touched her nose.

"For?"

She straightened to set her back against the pole. "Are you going to sit? Lap dance is extra."

"No." He could afford as many bespoke trousers as he needed, but he didn't throw them away by sitting in... He didn't care to identify what those stains were.

This was a ridiculous room. There was no space to

move without bumping into her. Nowhere to escape the enticing image of cheap, shiny polyester lying against the swells of firm, high breasts. He couldn't avoid the glimpse of her black bra, or the firm length of her tanned thighs encircled by those tantalizing garters. He wanted to tangle his fingers in them. Close his teeth on them.

"I was under the impression you were in a nursing program."

"I am. Part-time. Why? Is my birth father offended by my career choice?"

"He doesn't know." Axel hadn't known about it until he had landed and went to a bungalow in the suburbs to find her.

A matronly woman had answered the door, clutching her cardigan against the March wind as she studied him through round-rimmed glasses. *She's at work. Is there a problem?*

Axel had said it was a legal matter. Concerned, the woman had helpfully told him where to find her.

Even at that, Axel had assumed Joy was serving drinks, not dancing in a place called Martini's Cabaret. Not until he'd walked in and had his eyes nearly pulled from his skull by the raw sexuality she exuded.

He loathed feeling anything but completely in control of himself and his surroundings, but he hadn't been able to look away from her. She'd been mesmerizing. Bold in the way she met his gaze. His mind was still imprinted with the image of lithe, muscled limbs, the shimmy of her generously endowed chest and the flex of her firm, rounded buttocks.

Every time he met her hazel gaze, his sexual awareness of her ratcheted up another notch. Looking into her eyes tempted him to look at her mouth with her lush upper lip, and her long throat that he wanted to trace down to—

No.

"If you need money, you should have replied to my messages."

"Why would I do that when I can make you pay me to speak to you?" she mocked. "I get twenty percent off the fee for this room. Are you sure you don't want me to…?" In a move of supple power, she brought her knee up, then caught her arm under her calf to finish drawing her leg up, up, up until she was holding herself in the splits against the pole, hugging her raised leg and artfully dropping her other hand to grasp the pole exactly where his gaze most wanted to zero in.

She rolled her shoulder, and the robe slipped off her shoulder. A seductive smile drew itself across her lips.

A fresh zing of lust struck below his belt, one that dulled his brain and dimmed his vision. Before he realized what he was doing, he grasped the cool brass of the pole next to the ankle she held aloft. He leaned near enough that his nose was a millimeter from hers, close enough to feel the electricity between them.

Her breath hitched, and her lashes quivered, but she didn't move.

"No touching," she reminded, lips parted enticingly. Her gaze traveled over his face, scraping like sensual nails against his control, until her stare landed on his mouth.

He was nearly pulled off his feet but held himself

with steely discipline. "You want me to want you," he noted in a rasp. "You think that gives you power over me. I do want you."

Her startled gaze came back to his. Wariness entered her gaze, but a glow of wild excitement blossomed beneath it. That flare of reaction dug talons deeper into his libido, trying to drag it out to play.

"But I can wait until we've conducted our business," he continued, never breaking eye contact. "Can you?"

He let the beast in him steal one thorough look, all the way down to where the hem of her robe had ridden up to expose the tops of her thighs. To the narrow band of black that revealed she waxed to a Brazilian. Or less.

He was fully hard, if she cared to notice. The thud of his heart was a hammering pulse behind his fly.

In an abrupt move, she bent her upper leg around the pole, forcing him to take a step back or catch a spiked heel in the face. She seeming to defy gravity as she kicked her bottom leg out straight and spun in a slow circle, forcing him back another step, flashing him the frill that fluttered against the tops of her ass cheeks as she went by.

After three spins, she ended with both feet coming to rest on the floor.

"What I want," she said as she lifted her chin and set her shoulders back, "is for you to touch me so you'll get kicked out."

Lie. She was meeting his gaze, but her color was high. Her nipples were pebbled hard enough to show against the twin layers of bra cups and robe. It wasn't cold in here. Not at all. He was sweltering in his tie and jacket.

Damn it. This sexual pull between them was not something he'd factored into this arrangement, and he didn't have time to recalibrate. The stubborn street dog in him was fighting to take what was his. He was determined to beat Otto at his own game and quickly, especially now that Mira had partnered with a man who had his own ax to grind.

If Axel didn't take over Vorstoben soon, it might not be there at all.

He had wasted precious time trying to reach Joy through social media, then a couriered letter. She had ignored both. After asking Umberto if she'd responded to his messages, and hearing Umberto confirm she hadn't, Axel had invented an appointment in London and carried on here to Chicago to confront her in person.

"I don't have time for games," Axel stated. "I need you to take this seriously."

She stiffened at his commanding tone, but unsnaked her arm from around the pole, shifting so she grasped it behind her back.

"Would you take it seriously if you received messages like these?" she challenged. "My birth father wants to meet me, and I stand to inherit *hundreds* of millions of euros? Along with a company I have no idea how to run? And all I have to do is submit to a DNA test and show up in Germany? *Then* I will meet him and learn his name? Please," she dismissed the idea with scorn. "Would you like my bank details up front, so you can start pouring those millions into my account?"

She shifted her weight, causing her robe to slip a fraction of an inch, exposing more of her bra and a wider sliver of skin below it.

He dragged his gaze upward. "It's a delicate matter. He can't risk you selling the story before you've agreed to his narrative." Just as Axel couldn't risk her speaking to Otto first or tipping Otto off to his presence here. "I will need that DNA sample but…"

He told himself he was looking so closely at her features to compare her to the photo of Lorena as a young woman. Joy had her same arched brows and narrow, high-bridged nose. Her cheekbones were spaced with perfection in her oval face. Her lips were definitely her mother's, despite the makeup that made them seem fuller and plumper.

He didn't see much of Otto in her, thankfully, beyond her height and a feminine version of a mulish chin, which was good because he didn't want to kiss—

He bit back a curse. This was a business partnership he was courting. He had no intention of getting personal with her, let alone physical.

"But?" she prompted.

"Hmm?" DNA. Right. "Your birth name is Enja Fontaine, is it not?"

She tried not to react, but the way her expression blanked was its own tell.

"I'm confident you're the woman I'm looking for." A strange buzz arrived in his ears as he said that. He cleared his throat. "I don't have time to mollycoddle you. There's urgency around proving your identity and proceeding to the next steps."

Mira hadn't gone to the press yet, but she could. Revealing she was *not* Otto's biological daughter would embarrass him, which Otto deserved, but it could also harm her chances of getting at least a compulsory portion of his estate in the future.

Otto thought he had the upper hand with both of them, believing he could keep Axel on a leash while they waited for Joy to show up, but Axel wasn't waiting. Not anymore.

"Do you know what the top signs of fraud are?" Joy asked conversationally. "I looked them up. They include pretending to represent a family member…" she touched a fingertip, counting them off as she continued "…pressuring the victim to act quickly, asking for personal information—my DNA feels very personal—and asking the victim to spend their own money in order to get whatever is promised. Like paying for a DNA test?" She blinked her overly long, purple eyelashes before stating clearly, "No."

"I'll pay for the test. Maybe I'm wrong, and you're not her. There's only one way to find out, isn't there?"

"Are you hoping I'm not?" She smirked and looped her elbow around the pole, tilting her head against it. "What's wrong? Now that you've seen my profession, you're worried my father won't be so keen to meet me? How do I know who you're comparing my sample to, anyway? No." She shook her head. "It's too fishy."

"This won't affect his desire to meet you." Not when Axel introduced her as his wife and staked his claim on Vorstoben.

"But I haven't decided if I want to meet him." Her

playfulness dropped away, leaving a solemn expression that held no subterfuge whatsoever.

That was a wrinkle Axel hadn't anticipated. "You're not curious about him?"

"I was curious about my birth mother," she admitted. "But when I contacted the agency, all they could tell me was that she had already died. Which was a huge bummer." Dark shadows entered her eyes. "I knew that she didn't put my father's name on my birth certificate because he was married. I've always assumed that meant she didn't want him in my life or the other way around."

"That might have been true when she had you, but she signed an affidavit that was delivered to him after she died. I have a copy in my hotel room."

"Why didn't she want him to know about me until after she was gone?"

Spite, Axel suspected. Otto didn't invite many other emotions from those close to him. "His wife was pregnant at the time."

"I have a half sibling?" Her face brightened with wonder.

"No." Damn. For one second, she'd glowed with such delight, she'd hurt his eyes. Now all of that dimmed, and she glared at him as though he'd kicked her.

"Dead? See, this is why I don't want to do this. It's a roller coaster that I don't need." She looked to the door.

"His wife had a baby who isn't his. We'll get into all of that once I confirm your identity."

She shook her head. "If he's so interested in meeting me, why isn't he here himself?"

"There's a lot of money involved. It's complicated."

"And delicate." She threw his word back at him with ample mockery. "My life is also delicate and complicated. I have an ailing father who would be gutted to hear I have a rich birth father who wants to take his place. The person who was helping me with his care is pregnant with her second baby, so she moved closer to her own parents. That means my brother will go to California the next time he gets leave, rather than coming here. My sister-in-law was living with us, so we've lost her income, too. That leaves me covering the mortgage that Dad took out to cover his medical bills. My dancing keeps us sheltered and fed, so I can't go chasing waterfalls. Windfalls? Either way..." She rolled a dismissing shoulder. "Thanks, but no thanks."

"Prove you're his daughter, and your financial problems will be gone." He emphasized that with a cutting swipe of his hand through the air, still amazed himself with how many obstacles could be removed with the application of cash. "What would you do if you had unlimited funds? Move your father closer to your brother? Hire him a rotation of private nurses to offer care twenty-four-seven? I can start arranging that tonight."

"All you need is a vial of my blood?" she guessed with an acidic smile.

"I will pay you for a vial of your blood. How much do you want for it?" He had her now, and he would reel her in.

The last vestiges of sex kitten disappeared. She stood tall, arms folded, eyes narrowed with shrewdness, mouth firmed in deliberation. "I've been down this road, you know. I let a man snow me with false promises of a big payout, and now I'm dancing here instead of Broadway."

"Is that what you stand to lose if you leave with me tonight? This rewarding career of yours?" He sent a derisive look around the room. "I'm confident you can find similar employment if it turns out I'm wrong about you."

"You mean if *I'm* wrong about *you*." Her smile was a pained stretch of her lips.

"Take the test and find out."

"Twenty thousand dollars. Up front," she demanded.

He snorted. She'd already fleeced him for a room that couldn't be worth more than five hundred dollars for an hour, but he would have added a zero to her extortion figure if it meant he could claim Vorstoben. "Your money will be waiting with a nurse at my hotel. Let's go."

"Now?" she asked with alarm.

"Now."

CHAPTER FOUR

I CAN WAIT. Can you?

Joy hurried to the changing room, even more shaken than ever by her reaction to Axel Severin. Men wanted her all the time. She never wanted them. Not like this, but when he'd loomed over her in the Champagne Room, she'd been struck by an overwhelming urge to kiss him.

That would have been disturbing if he had been any stranger, but he was here on her birth father's behalf. She was beginning to believe that much, at least—that he was on a legitimate quest to find the offspring of Lorena Fontaine.

After losing Wendy, the mother who'd raised her, to a congenital heart problem, then learning the mother who'd birthed her was dead, Joy had shrunk inward. She'd tried to convince herself she didn't care where she came from. Her birth family didn't matter because her adoptive family loved her unconditionally. They had welcomed her home with open arms, hadn't they, after she'd made such a fool of herself over Todd?

Her disappointment over not being able to meet her birth mother had contributed to her falling for Todd's BS, though. She saw it clearly now that she had distance from it. She had been sad and adrift and had clung to the one close connection she'd had at the time. She had been so afraid to lose Todd, she'd put him above her own autonomy and aspirations, never seeing how one-sided and flimsy their relationship really was.

Now Axel was offering a new connection, one that he held just beyond her reach while saying, *I'm confident you're the woman I'm looking for.*

Her skin tightened as she remembered the specific timbre of his voice. She was still breathless and fluttery, still feeling accosted by his tightly contained energy and the sexual charisma that pierced her belly with yearning.

After removing her makeup, she quickly looked Axel up online, but only wound up with more questions than answers.

The first email about her birth father had come through the adoption agency. She'd been asked to reply to a lawyer called Umberto. She had still been deciding whether to respond and how to tell her father, Paul, about it when she'd received a private message from Axel through one of her social accounts.

She had blocked it, certain it was a bot. But receiving that message had made the one from the agency seem suspicious. When the couriered letter arrived two days later, she'd lied to her father and said it was about her student loans, but she'd been baffled and alarmed at the persistence of the scammers.

Axel wasn't a conman, though. Not according to the internet. Either he'd gone to great lengths to create this online persona or he was the CEO of a big infrastructure conglomerate in Germany.

If he was a CEO, what was he doing here, on her birth father's behalf?

She flicked through some photos of Axel. One showed him at a podium for a trade conference, another showed him arriving at a charity gala with his fiancée.

Fiancée!?

The sound of screeching brakes arrived in her ears, causing a sick lurch in her stomach.

Wow. Mira Braun was beautiful in an ultrasophisticated way. Even so, she didn't look particularly fulfilled wearing something that Joy presumed was a designer gown. Her sparkly earrings were probably real diamonds, and Axel wore a tuxedo, but they both wore similar, aloof expressions.

The photograph struck her as staged. Like the kind actors took with their costars when they secretly despised each other but had to do a press tour and act as though they were in love.

Maybe she was being uncharitable. Jealous, even. Of what, though? She didn't have any feelings toward Axel besides hostility. She sure as heck wasn't looking for love or romance. She was a complete cynic about those things, thanks to Todd. If anything, learning Axel was engaged filled her with contempt—and little surprise.

I do want you...

She shrugged her shoulders as a shiver chased down her spine.

Why were men such predictable jerks? And why was she attracted to him when he obviously was one?

She dropped her phone into her bag and finished dressing, pulling on jeans with short boots and a diamondknit pullover with a puffy jacket. She plopped a black motorcycle cap on her head and turned up her collar because the March wind off Lake Michigan was still cold enough to cut her in half.

She had half a mind to walk out the back door, but Axel was waiting in the hall, just inside the batwings.

"Ready?"

She clenched her teeth and followed him outside to a waiting SUV. He held the door for her, then directed the driver to the Ritz-Carlton.

The vehicle was tricked out like a limousine with a tiny refrigerator in the console between their armchairs. It held single-serve bottles of champagne and glass flutes along with a variety of snacks, including fresh fruit.

"Help yourself," he invited when he saw her taking inventory.

If this was a kidnapping—and she was only convinced it wasn't because she had nothing worth being ransomed for—she could see how easily Stockholm syndrome happened.

"I read that you're engaged," she said belligerently while fingering through playbills from the seat pocket, wistful that she wasn't in any of these musicals.

"It's been called off," he said dismissively.

"Convenient." She flicked him a glance of undisguised doubt.

He turned his head, face shadowed and unreadable. "It has."

The wall of derision she'd erected as a defense against him turned to sand. His masculine energy sparked and crackled in her direction again, licking like flames against her skin.

"You seem like a bigwig at a huge company." She changed tactics. "Why are you here, running errands for my father? Who is he to you?"

"We'll talk at the hotel."

So annoying.

They traveled in silence until they walked into the lobby of the hotel. A young man met them there. He wore a suit that rivaled Axel's and held a tablet inside a black leather cover.

"My assistant, Heskel. Ms. Youngston," Axel provided.

"It's nice to meet you, Ms. Youngston. Would you both come with me, please? Everything is ready upstairs." Heskel escorted them toward the elevators, speaking to Axel as they walked. "I made a reservation in the restaurant, but it's very busy. The chef has agreed to send something up if you prefer?"

"Three courses with a paired wine," Axel said with an absent nod.

As they stepped into the elevator, Heskel opened his tablet cover and extracted something. "For you, Ms. Youngston." He offered a slim red leather sleeve that held what looked like a single credit card.

She didn't take it, only moved her gaze from the card to Axel's impassive expression.

"You asked for twenty thousand dollars," Axel said. "That's preloaded with thirty, to assist with legal costs. You'll want someone you can trust."

Heskel continued holding out the card like a barker on the street, trying to entice passersby into his peep show.

Axel plucked the card, then picked up her hand and pressed the card against her palm, folding her fingers around it.

No touching, she thought, even as fireworks shot through her. His hands were warm. Strong and insistent. Magical in their ability to halt the elevator midair. To stop the earth from rotating and make her feet leave the floor.

We called it off.

A vibration between longing and apprehension arrived in her breastbone, sending skittering sensations into the depths of her abdomen. The vibration dropped low, like embers that stayed hot and heavy in the notch of her thighs.

She yanked her hand away and shoved the card into the back pocket of her jeans. "Must be nice, being able to arrange something like this at the drop of a text," she said, using a snotty tone because she was so disconcerted.

"You'll soon find out, won't you?"

The elevator doors opened, and Axel waved her to exit first.

Joy had been working up her courage to have her blood drawn. She hated needles, but it turned out to be a cheek swab. She had barely removed her hat and jacket before the nurse was leaving with the sample, Heskel on her heels.

Blinking with astonishment, Joy suddenly found herself alone with Axel. This time there was no bouncer beyond the door or a CCTV to record what happened between them.

"Happy?" She rose and touched the credit card in her back pocket, wondering if it would really work. She reached for her jacket where it was draped over the arm of the sofa.

"Wait." He picked up the card the nurse had left on the coffee table, the one with Joy's file number written on it. "Email Umberto. Tell him you've sent your sample to this lab and give him this number. Tell him that when you receive confirmation that it's a match, you'll make arrangements to travel to Germany to meet your father. It's the middle of the night there, but he'll see it first thing. By the time you wake here, you'll know."

"Give you an inch, and you take a mile, don't you?" she muttered as she dug in her bag for her phone.

"What is that in metric?" he asked with false interest.

"A crap ton of arrogance," she provided with a sweet smile. "I can't just drop everything and fly to Germany, you know. I have responsibilities." Even so, she took the card and sank back onto the sofa while she began to scroll through her trashed emails.

"All of that will be taken care of. Don't mention me in the message."

"Why not?" She looked up.

"Because I asked you not to."

She snorted. Arrogance didn't begin to cover his brashness. "This all sounds very shady. Are you making me an accomplice in something illegal?"

"No."

"As if you would admit to it," she grumbled.

"I will explain after you send the message." He took on a tone of weary patience and walked over to the bar. "Would you like something before dinner arrives?"

"What is this, a date now? Because I don't care how much money is on the credit card. You paid for a test and a conversation."

"Then make the test happen, and we'll continue our conversation." He didn't even look at her, only focused on unboxing a bottle of scotch.

Dictator.

She found the email from the agency and typed her response to Umberto, reading it aloud before she sent it. "My sample number is yada yada at the lab yada yada. Once a match is confirmed, we can discuss a meeting with my birth father." She looked to Axel for confirmation.

"Perfect. Thank you."

She hit Send, and the whoosh filled the quiet room.

He poured a finger's worth of amber liquid into a glass. "None for you?" he asked again.

"No. Thank you." She stood as nerves arrived with a return of her crackling awareness that she was alone with him. It had been different in the private room at the club. She always felt confident in her costume. Yes, it left her mostly naked, but it was still a type of mask, one that gave her a certain power.

Wearing her worn, dated jeans and thrift-store sweater was a different type of revealing. Things had been financially dismal before she'd moved home and discovered her father's coffers were also empty.

She moved to the window. The luxurious corner suite was one of the hotel's finest with a full-size lounge, a dining table for six and views of Navy Pier. Out on the black lake, the pinprick lights of ships bobbed like untethered stars.

"Don't results take a few days?" she asked over her shoulder.

"Not when you pay for a lab tech to remain on standby."

Axel's level of wealth was hitting her like a wrecking ball. Or rather, the fact that he didn't seem to need to squeeze money out of an overdrawn exotic dancer from a very middling middle-class family. It made all of this more distressingly real.

"Tell me about your relationship to my birth father." She turned to see he'd taken a seat facing her.

His gaze came up from her jean pockets. Even though half the room separated them and neither of them moved, she had the sense of the walls shrinking inward and him coming up against her. It was a wild rush of heat that curled around her, pulling her close. Caging her.

Her heart lurched, and a sting exploded in her chest, rising into her throat and blossoming in her cheeks. She pretended it wasn't happening and lifted a brow in challenge.

He tilted his head in a self-deprecating, *You caught me*.

But there was no sheepishness in him. He was too direct, letting her see the power and ferocity within him. The desire.

She heard his graveled voice again. *I do want you. But I can wait.*

Her stomach swooped. It should have been with alarm, but it was the vertigo of being on a swing with her eyes closed or the uneven, hysterical thrill of being swept along whitewater rapids.

"My information on you was incomplete." He sipped his drink. "I didn't know about your side hustle. That leads me to wonder what else I don't know. Are you involved with anyone?"

"What *do* you know about me?" She crossed her arms, not liking how easily he put her on her back foot. Did he know about Todd? "Have you been having me followed?"

"No. I glanced over your social profiles." He spoke dismissively, as though it should be obvious that was all anyone needed to do. "You began your degree in performing arts with a focus on modern dance but quit in your third year. You were living with someone at the time but moved home last year, possibly because of your father's declining health? Parkinson's, is it?"

"Yes." She had come home for his birthday and realized how badly Carrie was struggling to work around caring for a toddler and an adult who needed increasing levels of assistance.

Since she had already dropped out of school, and Todd was bleeding her dry, Joy had cut her losses. She had told Todd she wasn't coming back to Connecticut. He'd squeezed one final month of rent out of her and kept the good coffee maker, but eventually sent her a box of her things, COD. of course.

"You've since enrolled in a nursing program," Axel

continued. "Presumably because it's a stable career that would allow you to help your father. Your brother is an air force pilot with a wife, a small child and another baby on the way. You like animal videos and avoid political content. You don't advertise your alter ego or where you perform."

"Gee, I wonder why, when strangers show up and admit to stalking me."

"I'm not a very good stalker if I don't know whether you have a boyfriend, am I? Do you?" he pressed.

"Why? Does my birth father expect him to ask permission to date me?"

"No. I do."

"Ha!"

He only sipped his drink, reeking of patience while her heart galloped in her chest. How did he look so damned sexy and, yes, dangerous, sitting there relaxed and watchful?

"Silly me, I thought whom I date would be my choice."

"You would think, but we've both been pushed into a corner." He looked into his glass, tilting the liquid this way and that. "I'd like to put my cards on the table, Joy. It's more expedient, rather than waiting until we have the test result. If I do that, I want your assurance that what I tell you will stay in this room." His gaze came up.

"Or?"

"Or you will be made very uncomfortable. That's not a threat. It's the truth. Your birth father has a high enough profile there would be significant publicity. Whatever you might make in selling this story, you would spend on hiring a PR agency and personal security to manage the fallout."

"Good grief, who is he?"

"Do I have your word?"

"Fine. Yes." She glanced toward the bedroom. "There's probably a Bible in here if you need me to swear on it. But please, for the love of all that's holy, tell me what's going on."

"We'll need that Bible," he said with a faint quirk of his lips. "I'm here to marry you."

CHAPTER FIVE

She barked out a laugh. Because he had to be joking. How could he not be?

"With a sturdy prenup," he said as though he hadn't blurted out something so absurd she had already dismissed it. "After a year, we'll quietly divorce and go back to our separate lives."

"This conversation has officially jumped the shark." She walked across to pick up her bag and jacket again.

"You promised to listen."

She removed the credit card from her jean pocket and left it on the coffee table.

He picked up a manila envelope from the end table and dropped it next to the credit card. It landed with a slap.

She froze. "What is that?" she asked suspiciously.

"The letter from your birth mother to your father." He sat back. "And a list of assets you're in line to inherit along with a copy of the contract that proves you *will* inherit the lion's share of your birth father's fortune if you marry me. You'll be very wealthy, Joy."

"I don't care for this judgy attitude of yours." She waggled her finger at him. "Acting like I'm driven solely by money."

"I don't judge you for that." His brow quirked as though he was affronted by the accusation. "Everyone is driven by money to some extent. I'm here because I want the piece of your fortune that was promised to me. Sit down." He nodded at the sofa. "Let me explain."

She told her feet to take her to the door, but the envelope and its secrets called to her. She inched back to stand on the far side of the coffee table from him, arms folded, staring down at the envelope as though it contained a viper that would slither out and sink its fangs into her. But she was too fascinated by its sway to look away.

"Your father is Otto Braun."

"The father of your fiancée." She lifted her surprised gaze to his.

"Ex," he corrected. "And he's not her father. But you've got the gist of it." He leaned forward to set down his glass and opened the envelope. He shook out its contents across the tabletop. Catching at the corner of a photo, he drew it away from the rest, pushing it toward her.

She picked up the photo and studied the man who was well-kempt with a longish face and a neatly trimmed white beard. He carried some middle-age weight and his features were lined by age. He was handsome, but there was a certain hardness to his expression.

Was this really where she had come from? She slowly sank onto the sofa, feeling porous and suddenly needing to absorb everything Axel could tell her.

He reached forward again and pushed a photograph of a woman toward her. "Lorena Fontaine. French. She moved to New York when she became pregnant and returned to Europe a few years later."

Joy picked up the dated photo of a woman taken when Lorena was close to Joy's twenty-four. She was elegant in a timeless way, wearing a dress with chiffon sleeves and holding a cigarette in two fingers. Her lips were tilted in a half smile around a whistling exhale of smoke, as though she was amused by whoever was taking her photo.

Joy recognized enough of herself in the woman's features to feel knocked off her equilibrium. Her body reacted as though she'd been pushed or struck or grabbed. Her blood was singing with adrenaline, urging her to run. Or fight.

"This is her letter to your father. They rekindled their affair about five years after your birth. His wife was still alive then." He found a photocopy of a handwritten letter and offered it to her. A notarized translation into English was stapled behind it. "Lorena says she knew he wouldn't forgive her for giving you up, but when she was diagnosed with lung cancer, she decided to tell him about you. I don't see any reason she would lie about him being your father. Not if she was waiting until after her death to inform him. What did she have to gain?"

He fell silent while Joy scanned the translation. There wasn't much more to it than what he had just said. Lorena mentioned the name of the adoption agency and hoped that Otto would *provide your daughter the lifestyle she ought to have had*.

Joy had always felt like she was her birth mother's dirty little secret. Learning that Lorena had waited until after her death to tell her father reinforced that impression, sending a deep pang into her heart.

"Does she have any family? Do they know about me?" she asked, trying to keep the husk from her voice.

"I couldn't say. Her parents are gone, but her brother is still alive. I have no idea if that's something she would have shared with him."

"Especially if she wasn't even telling her baby's father." Joy frowned, trying to understand. Trying not to be stung by her complete erasure from her blood relatives' lives.

"Given the timing of their second affair, my suspicion is that Otto had recently learned his wife had also had an affair. The child he believed was his daughter was not."

"Mira." She lowered Lorena's photo into her lap.

"Yes. Until I learned that, I couldn't understand Otto's ambivalence toward her." Axel was doing a good job of seeming completely impassive, but a muscle ticked in his cheek. "I don't imagine Otto was in a mood to hear he had a biological daughter he couldn't claim. I'm guessing that's why Lorena didn't tell him and wound up breaking things off again."

"But now he knows and wants to meet me?" She was having trouble controlling her expression, feeling her mouth wobbling toward a smile even as her chin crinkled anxiously.

"I'll be frank with you, Joy." He leaned forward, and his hard voice gave her inner child a pinch on the arm, then twisted it. "Otto wants to use you to keep me at Vorstoben."

She frowned. "Isn't that what you want?"

"Not exactly." He picked up his drink and sat back.

"I want to quit working for him and work for myself. I told him two years ago that I was leaving to open my own firm. I wasn't intending to compete directly with him. Vorstoben takes on complex, billion-dollar projects. Factories and resorts. I've always seen a need for highly skilled, bespoke services. Projects that are challenging in a different way. When I told him I was leaving, Otto promoted me to CEO. He said he would retire once I married his daughter and gift us the company after a year of marriage. He let me believe all this time that his daughter was Mira."

"Oh." Until Axel said that, his proposal had been a joke. Now the determination she read in him was rolling over her like a cool, frothy tide. It should have frozen her to the bone, but it rocked her while sand shifted beneath her feet. Nothing was solid. She was being tossed around and tugged out to sea.

Tugged by a god who would not take no for an answer.

That's been called off. You're the woman I'm looking for.

Her heart began to thud as though he was pursuing her through the dark city streets.

"I agreed to his offer." He was still holding her gaze, filling her ears with the smooth timbre of his voice. "I poured myself into Vorstoben, believing it would be mine as soon as Mira and I married. He wouldn't let us set a date. Wouldn't finalize the terms." He took a gulp of scotch and bared his teeth at the burn. "A month ago, I said I wouldn't wait any longer. He offered me this." He took up a slim envelope from the pile and unfolded what looked like a contract of several pages. "It promises that if I marry his *biological* daughter, he'll honor the terms he set two years ago. That was when Mira and I both learned she isn't his daughter. And that you are."

"That's how he told her?" She didn't know Mira, but she felt the other woman's shock on a visceral level, and the unmooring sensation it must have caused her. "That's horrible. Why do you even work for someone who acts like that?"

"Call it a deep need to express myself through executive movement," he said with heavy sarcasm. "He gave me opportunities and valuable experience when I needed it. That inspired a certain loyalty in me, but you're right. He's not nice. On the other hand, he's made it clear he won't leave the company to Mira, so I'm not trying to steal it from her. I only want what he promised me."

"I don't understand how you think he could use me, though?"

"He'll offer you his fortune if you marry me," he said simply and pointed at the contract. "He knows damned well that you would feel this hesitancy you're showing. Who would marry a stranger? It's a ridiculous ask."

"Thank you." These were the first sensible words he'd said all night.

"He would use your reservation to string me along, but I've reached the end of my forbearance. According to this contract…" he gave the pages a ruffle "…upon marrying me, Otto's *biological* daughter stands to inherit all of this." He filtered through the papers again and showed her a list of properties. The value tallied up to a hefty nine figures. The largest asset was Vorstoben, making up more than half.

Joy almost swallowed her tongue.

"I imagine Lorena felt some guilt at denying you the fortune you were entitled to inherit, once she realized Otto was balking at leaving it to Mira."

"But that's adoption." Joy shot to her feet and paced away in agitation. "You can drive yourself crazy thinking about the life you might have had if you had been raised by your birth mother. I'm really happy with the upbringing I had, though." Wendy hadn't been able to get pregnant again after having David. She had longed for a daughter, and Joy had arrived days after David started school. Joy had had her full, doting attention. "Mom and I were super close. That's why I waited until she was gone to even contact the agency. I've never had fantasies that anyone would come along and *rescue* me."

"Good. That's not why I'm here."

"No, you want to marry me to get your hands on things that aren't even mine!" She waved at the table.

"Only Vorstoben." He swallowed the last of his drink and sucked his teeth. "I already own a number of shares in it. Once I gain the ones that contract awards me, I will be the majority shareholder, which grants me total control. So I won't let him renege. Not again."

"But that comes at *my* expense. I don't want to be used by either of you." She shook her head, honestly wondering if she'd taken some of that weird cough medicine that gave her squirrely dreams. "No. There's no reason for me to agree to any of this."

At that moment, the door lock hummed. Heskel stepped inside and held the door open for the room service trolley to be pushed in by a server. As the server began setting the table, Heskel gave Joy a diffident nod.

"I apologize for the interruption, Ms. Youngston, but I have a few questions regarding your father's care. Is there any interest in a full-service senior building? There's one located near your sister-in-law that seems very well recommended. The cost is comparable to purchasing and retrofitting a home for accessibility, then hiring appropriate staff, so I thought it makes sense to explore it?"

"Puh... Pardon? I haven't agreed to anything." She threw that at Axel, alarmed.

"This is for discussion purposes." Axel rose and set aside his empty glass. "Heskel is pulling together options to present to your father. You seemed concerned that your brother will visit your father less often, now that his wife lives across the country. I asked Heskel to include a plan that moves your father closer to his grandchildren. If he chooses to stay in his current home and have a nurse come daily, that's up to him, but with my resources you can offer more far-reaching solutions."

"But I don't have your resources. Not unless—"

"Exactly," Axel cut in. "Include it," he instructed Heskel. "With a timeline on when the move could be accomplished."

"Of course. I'll be across the hall. Please text if you need anything." Heskel accepted the bill from the server and signed it, then followed the server out the door.

Axel drew out a chair for Joy at the dining table.

She sat as though in a trance, mind incapable of grasping a solid thought. She was halfway through the soup course before its delicate taste traveled from her tongue to her brain. Even then, she couldn't have said if she liked it.

"I'm probably not even her." At this point, she didn't know if a negative result would be a relief or a devastating loss.

The server had lit a candle. The soft glow painted flickers of golden light against Axel's cheekbones and brow and mouth. His eyelids blinked once, slowly. Almost suggesting pity at how she was grasping at straws.

"You'll still have thirty thousand dollars and a story you can never tell," he said dryly.

She choked slightly and pulled her spoon from her mouth. "Lucky me."

Thirty thousand dollars was not chump change, but it would only give her breathing space. Deeper pockets could alter the course of her father's care altogether, vastly improving the quality of his golden years.

She rowed her spoon in her soup.

"Could I really afford to move Dad into a senior building?" she asked tentatively. "A *nice* one?" Because she'd seen the ones she could afford, and it was another reason she'd started dancing at Martini's.

Triumph flashed in Axel's fierce blue eyes, telling her she'd tipped her hand, but it was too late to backtrack now. "The level of care you can offer him will astound you," he assured her.

He was stepping right on her Achilles' heel. She knew he was manipulating her with her emotions because it had happened once before. This time was different, though. It wasn't about her fearing abandonment. It was actually a fierce desire to give back to the man who had raised her and given her a warm and loving upbringing. Paul might be dependent on her now, but for most of her life he had been her safety net. He had done his best to give her a solid foundation to launch from. It wasn't his fault she had flubbed it.

"All I have to do is marry you?" she asked tentatively. "And meet my birth father?"

"We have to stay married a year. You'll behave as my wife in public."

"Where do you live?" she asked curiously.

"Vorstoben's head office is in Berlin, but I have a number of residences that you can retreat to. We don't have to live in each other's pockets."

A number of residences...

It was mind-boggling. Nothing about this made sense.

"What about..." Her voice dried up.

His attention lifted from his plate and settled on her in a way that was almost as physical as feeling him press her into a mattress. He was attractive. She couldn't help but be aware of that. She could cut her finger on the edge of his jaw, and those masculine lips would kiss it better.

Her pulse fluttered at the mere idea of his lips against her fingertip.

She looked away, embarrassed. She'd never experienced anything so carnal. An inappropriate fantasy of walking around the table and straddling his lap came into her head. He looked strong enough to pick her up and carry her to the sofa from there.

The corners of his mouth dug in, making her think he could see her thoughts like he was watching a film.

She couldn't tell if he was amused or satisfied or if that reaction was something more reciprocal.

"When I said I want you, I meant it." His gaze slid to her mouth, and her blood turned to fire.

She knew when men were ogling her, and this wasn't that. He wasn't looking at her like a source for his sexual pleasure. He was looking at her with a mixture of intent and appreciation. As though they already had secrets between them. Delectable, seductive secrets.

"I'd rather you came to me with your own wants." His features took on a more concrete implacability. "Managing public opinion around your recent occupation will be difficult enough without you partaking in extracurriculars."

"Excuse me," she blustered, erotic thoughts scorched away by an indignant blush. "You're making a lot of assumptions. I don't partake in extracurriculars. I dance for money, but that's all I do for it. I don't go home with men. Not for money or recreation. So don't presume you can take possession of *me* along with everything else you think I can get for you."

"I'm only making clear that if you do have an itch, you'll come to me to scratch it."

"Keep dreaming," she muttered but only got an unimpressed mouth twitch in response. "I haven't even agreed to marry you, in case you haven't noticed."

"I noticed." He switched out their soup for the entrees, lamb chops with asparagus and cherry tomatoes atop ravioli. The sauce smelled like mint. "What else do you need besides the arrangements for your father? I can pay off your student loans."

"That's what the credit card is for." Those loans had been hanging over her like an anvil on a fraying rope, but they were hers to pay. Actually, they were Todd's, but paying them off was a punishment to herself for being so stupid. She wouldn't make them anyone else's problem.

"I'll clear them along with your father's mortgage. Call it a wedding gift. Shall we discuss your allowance?"

"I'm not twelve."

"Stipend? What do you want to call it? It's only for budgeting purposes. You'll have leeway to overshoot it."

"You're moving too fast," she muttered.

"I told you there was urgency. Let's find the clincher." He set his elbows on the table and laced his fingers together, imposing his iron will upon her. "If you could have anything you wanted in the world, right now, what would it be?"

"I don't know." She couldn't imagine a life without all these stressors and obligations that had been accumulating for years.

But as she sighed and looked into the flickering flame on the candle, her heart wrenched with yearning toward the one thing she'd been pretending she was okay with losing. The thing she sought and found, in a watered-down form at least, whenever she walked onstage and grasped the pole. The one place where she had always felt she belonged.

The words came out of her like an incantation. "I want to dance."

His brows shot up.

"To finish my degree," she clarified crossly. "I want to

perform with musicians and artists." For a real audience, not a bunch of men looking to scratch their own itch.

She'd lost so much time on that aspiration. It broke her heart to consider where she might be if she hadn't let Todd derail her. Dancing at Martini's had been as much about regaining the condition of her body and rejuvenating her skills as filling the coffers because, deep down, she secretly dreamed of returning to dance. Somehow. Even though it seemed impossible.

Axel picked up his phone. "I'll put Heskel onto researching academies."

"No. It's..." Against her best judgment, her heart lifted with anticipation. Hope.

She hadn't allowed herself to feel that emotion in so long, it brought a sting of tears into her eyes. If she had a chance to train again, she should take it. Shouldn't she? Before age and all the other vagaries of life made it even less likely that she could?

"What about the wedding itself?" he asked as though she'd agreed. "I'd prefer simple, but if you have your heart set on something bigger—"

"For a fake marriage? No," she scoffed.

But there was one girlish dream she had all but abandoned. One that she saw could still come true *if* she acted soon. Oh, he was cruel to offer this to her when it meant everything to her and their marriage would mean nothing.

Still.

"I want..." She had to swallow the thickness from her throat. "I want my father walk me down the aisle. My real one. Paul."

"Of course. Let me relay that to Heskel." He tapped his phone.

She was still reeling from how easy he made all of this sound when his phone pinged.

He read the reply. "Heskel says we can marry twenty-four hours after we purchase the license. We'll do that first thing tomorrow morning, so we can marry Thursday. We'll fly overnight and meet Otto on Friday morning."

"Wait. What?" Her heart nearly came out her mouth. "I haven't even told my father that Otto reached out." She rose, truly needing to run away from all of this. It wasn't real. It couldn't be.

"Would you like me to speak to him with you?"

The way he was capable of railroading a person? Her poor father wouldn't know what had hit him.

"No." She hurried across to pick up her jacket and pushed her arms into it. "This will hurt his feelings. His condition has taken a downturn lately, and he's not rich like Otto. I don't want him to feel like he failed me or anything." She needed a couple of tries to close the zipper on her jacket. "I don't care about the money." She lifted her face and looked him in the eye as she said it, so he would know it was the absolute truth. "I want to meet my birth father to satisfy my curiosity about where I came from. I don't have to marry you to do that."

It was a reminder to him and herself that she still held agency in this situation.

"True," Axel agreed, picking up her hat and all the documents from the table, bringing everything to her, including the credit card. "Read the contract, though. Otto expects you to marry me if you want to inherit from him. If you go to him without me, I will refuse."

She felt struck by that bluntness. There was such a lethal finality in his voice, it emptied her chest while opening two paths before her. She had the same feeling she'd had when she had dropped out of school. She had known she would regret it. She had known she wouldn't be able to go back to that moment and take the path she *really* wanted.

Which path did she really want today?

"If Otto sees that you're no use to him, he'll discard you. You'll be back in the cabaret within the week," Axel warned in that dispassionate tone.

"I'm not afraid of that," she claimed, even though she wished every day that she didn't have to be there.

"Then don't be afraid to accept a bigger payout for an easier gig," he said tersely.

Her backbone lost some of its steel. She took her hat and set it on her head, then accepted the papers from him.

"Joy." He gave her hat a slight adjustment, centering it, then smoothed her hair back from her temples.

He was barely touching her, but it sent tickling frissons of sensation through her shoulder blades. The pleasure was at odds with the apprehension she felt when she studied the hard angles of his expression.

"I want your allegiance." His gaze locked with hers. "I will only know I have it if I've purchased it before you meet him. You don't know yet how badly you need my protection from him, but you do. So give me your promise now. If the test proves you're his daughter, you'll marry me before you speak to him."

"We met two hours ago," she protested. "You want to marry me in *two* days." Her voice cracked.

His expression didn't change.

She searched his eyes, wishing she knew whether she could trust him. She wouldn't know until she did, though.

Which was how she had learned that she couldn't trust Todd.

She *wanted* to believe in Axel, though. That was a very alarming realization when she had pretty much sworn off trusting any man after Todd.

What Axel was proposing could break apart what was left of her life. Or he might help her rebuild it so it was strong and unshakable. He was making her a very alluring offer when she didn't know how she would manage another few months, let alone years of carrying so much financial baggage and a parent who was growing more dependent on her.

Maybe she wanted her troubles to be washed away with money and maybe she wanted to dance again. But she knew, deep down, that she wanted something else, too.

She was fighting against acknowledging it but had to face it when he touched her chin, urging her to lift her gaze. A hot streak of sensuality ran down her throat.

He was attractive and intriguing and powerful and inscrutable.

She tried to swallow but couldn't. She wanted to close her eyes and hide. But couldn't. She wanted him to kiss her with those wickedly beautiful lips.

"Do I have your word?" he asked gravely.

Her heart was beating so hard and fast, she nodded as an escape tactic, so he would release her.

"I'm probably not her anyway," she repeated in a thin voice.

"We'll know soon."

He took her home. They didn't speak beyond, "Good night," and, "You have my number."

Her father was already asleep. She sneaked into her bed and read through everything Axel had given her, then tossed and turned until her phone pinged at three in the morning.

It was an email from Umberto with the test results.

Probability of paternity: 99.9999%

She stared at it for a long time before she sent it to Axel.

Even though it was the middle of the night, he texted back immediately.

I'll be there at nine to buy our license.

CHAPTER SIX

AXEL REFUSED TO check his watch.

Aside from how it would affect his battle with Otto, being left at the altar was not something that would bother him too much. The only guest was his bride's father, who wasn't here yet because he was coming with Joy. The ceremony was being held in a quiet, hundred-year-old mansion on the lakeshore. An equally small brunch would be wasted, but most of what Axel had spent on bribing Joy to agree to this marriage could be stopped or recouped.

Axel had never aspired to marry anyway, not until Otto had made it a vehicle to getting something he wanted. Agreeing to marry Mira had been an easy choice. A safe one. Until the last time he'd seen her, Mira had always been even-keeled and cooperative. Axel had liked that about her. She had never riled more emotion out of him than sympathy or a snort of amusement at one of her facetious comments.

Marrying Joy would not be that inert.

Which bothered him. He had been shoved around by life enough that he no longer allowed it. Coming here to marry Otto's "real" daughter was him grabbing the wheel on his future, refusing to be driven by anyone's will but his own.

Yet here he was, tying himself to a woman who was already igniting more reaction in him than he'd allowed himself to feel in years.

It was sexual, of course. He couldn't get the vision of her undulating, nearly naked body out of his head. He had had to take himself in hand more than once over the last day and a half just to be able to think.

But she was scrappy, too, not giving ground easily. It was annoying to come up against. He'd risen to a level where few people pushed back on him, but he couldn't help but respect her for it. She would need that feistiness, given what he was asking of her.

He was asking a lot, he had realized, once he met her father and saw how severely Paul was impacted by his condition.

"I told him we've been dating a while," Joy had confided yesterday when he had arrived to take her to the courthouse for their license. "I said I hadn't mentioned you because I wasn't sure how serious we were, but that you asked me to come live with you in Europe. I said I would only go with you if you married me first, so you proposed. I didn't mention Otto." She grimaced at the lies and omissions. "I didn't want to fully stop his heart."

They had detoured through a jewelry shop on their way back to the house. Joy had looked at modest solitaires, but Axel had picked out a three-stone engagement ring with channel-set baguettes down the shank. The band was a matching design.

Then he played the part of a doting bridegroom when she introduced him to Paul. That had given him the excuse to hold her hand and touch her waist, and he'd found it entirely too gratifying to see goose bumps rise on her arm when he did.

Her reaction made it easy to convince her father that they were smitten and *had* to be together, but Axel didn't like how much he felt it within himself. Each minute he spent with her planted another seed of want in him. Another fantasy of having her in his bed every night.

After a childhood of wanting things he couldn't have, he'd hardened himself against needing much. He liked his creature comforts—who didn't?—and he was willing to work hard to afford them, but aside from food, water and shelter, he didn't *need* anything.

He didn't need this marriage, he insisted to himself. Especially to a woman who provoked such prickly discord in him. Such want. He'd be better off if she didn't show up.

In a failure of willpower, he dragged his brooding gaze off the black marble of the fireplace and looked over his shoulder.

Heskel hurried up to him from his position by the door. He lowered his voice as though there was an audience of guests when there was only the pianist and the officiant, both of whom had given up trying to make small talk with Axel and were speaking to each other in hushed tones on the other side of the room.

"I just had a text from the driver," Heskel said. "There was a delay leaving the house. Her brother called. Explanations had to be made. They'll be here shortly."

Axel nodded, and Heskel went back to his position.

Axel ignored the pound of his relieved pulse in his ears. He told himself he was only pleased he would get what he'd been striving for most of his life: true self-reliance.

Too much of his life had been lived in circumstances he couldn't control, answering to people with more power than he had.

Why do you work for someone like that?

Axel's sarcastic reply about working his own pole had been all too true. He had grasped what was available in order to pull himself up.

His parents had been children themselves, ill-equipped to raise him. There'd been drugs and arguing and petty crimes even before his father had been killed in a bar fight. Axel had had no say when he was taken away and given back to his mother. The foster system might have ensured he had clean clothes and vouchers for food, but he'd been disparaged for being a drain on the system. For being poor.

At twelve, desperate for money that didn't involve following his parents into unsavory means, he'd lied about his age and got his first job pushing a broom at a building site. His coworkers, grown men, had laughed at him, calling him a weed and a bookworm because he never laughed and scribbled through his homework while eating a jelly sandwich in two bites like a feral dog.

But he'd been able to keep his landlord from evicting them from the squalid room they occupied and that had been something.

Learn a trade, a bricklayer had advised him when he was fourteen and showing competence at anything he was taught. He'd been strong in math and already understood drawings and building principles. He applied to a trade school at sixteen, thinking to become an electrician, but the career counselor at school had encouraged him to aim higher.

So he'd studied engineering. Between his university classes and his night watchman job, he interned at Vorstoben, specializing in industrial projects. They hired him full-time the day he graduated with honors.

Axel hadn't rested on his laurels. He continued his education, taking a master's degree in business management, drawing the attention of his superiors. Eventually, the big man himself had noticed him.

Otto's mentorship had meant something to him. No one else had backed him in the same way. He had been loyal to Otto. That was what made Otto's bait-and-switch betrayal so galling.

That was what made Axel so determined to get what he had been promised.

Voices murmured at the entryway. Heskel nodded at the pianist to take her seat and for the officiant to stand before Axel, then he opened the pair of doors wide.

Gentle notes began to fill the room.

Axel's bride entered, and all his ire and grim memories evaporated.

Nothing about her appearance was extravagant. Her makeup was far more understated than the night he'd met her. Her gown was a creamy satin that draped in a slim column down her graceful form. Her sleeves fell in folds off her shoulders, leaving her upper chest bare but for a silver locket that looked like an heirloom. Her hair fell in big curls held back from her face with a band of white flowers. Her bouquet was only three peach-colored roses with a sprig of greenery.

She was undeniably beautiful, but her true beauty was in the way she looked at her father. The expression on her face wrapped a fist around Axel's lungs and squeezed. *That's love*, he thought as she walked slowly, very slowly, alongside her father's struggling, lopsided gait. Axel had never seen such a blatant display of that particular emotion. He wouldn't have known how to recognize it, if he hadn't had the context of knowing how much that man meant to her.

Guilt pinched his conscience. He had extorted her cooperation by leaning heavily on her love for her father, thinking nothing of taking her away from the warm fold of her family and dropping her into a war zone.

Otto would never look at her the way Paul did, with pride and tender affection.

Joy glanced at Axel, sending another punch into his chest because her expression shone with poignant gratitude. *I want my father to walk me down the aisle.*

Of all the things he'd bribed her with, this was the one that meant the most to her? A strange lump formed in his throat, one he reflexively cleared, pushing away sentiment.

This marriage was a means to an end for both of them. That was all.

Joy and Paul arrived before him. She stooped so her father could kiss her cheek, then watched him shuffle to his seat before she faced Axel again.

Now there was somberness in her pouted mouth and trepidation in her eyes. The petals on her bouquet trembled.

All Axel could think was that he wanted to touch her. Seize her.

A prickle of alarm went through him. He never allowed himself to feel anything deeply, but this was intense and carnal and sharp. Chaotic. He wanted to claim her as badly—maybe more—than the things their marriage would gain him.

Which should have been a red flag.

It was.

But he ignored it.

"You look beautiful," he told her, then ordered the officiant, "Begin."

"Thank you for being here today," the officiant began.

Run, the adrenaline in Joy's veins kept urging.

Call it off, her brother had insisted, not buying for a second that she'd been having a secret affair with a foreign tycoon. *What the hell is really going on?*

She didn't know. It had all happened so fast. The twenty-four hours she might have used for second thoughts had been eaten up by lawyer visits and interviewing nursing staff and shopping for a dress.

"I have the chance to meet my birth father," she had admitted in a whisper to David behind the locked door of her bedroom.

"You don't have to marry a stranger to do that."

I want to. She hadn't said it, but there was a trapped bird inside her that kept batting its wings against her rib cage, panicked and urgent and, for some reason, trying to fly straight to Axel.

Which didn't make sense. She knew it didn't. Especially when she stood before him and the ceremony started and each word inched her further and further toward the end of the proverbial plank. Soon she would be over the edge, plummeting into a bottomless ocean that was miles over her head.

Axel's voice dropped deep into his chest as he made his vows to honor and respect her, to build a marriage that would grow stronger and more caring as time passed, blanketing her in a belief that he meant it.

Her chest filled with currents and eddies as she repeated the words to him, feeling dizzy. The vows felt real, the ring weighty as he slid it onto her finger. His gaze flashed with satisfaction as he did it, and her knees grew weak.

This was a business deal. He was doing this to get a company, she reminded herself, blinking against silly, emotive tears. If she felt an urge to cry, it was only because she hadn't slept.

"You may seal your bond with a kiss."

He drew her into his arms, and she stiffened, trying not to give in to whatever this force was that had taken possession of her deepest self. She lifted her mouth, expecting a brush of his lips in a chaste observance of tradition.

But as the strength in his arms and the warmth of his thighs penetrated her gown, this unnamed, shimmering grip he had on her coiled tighter around her. It changed her, molding her to a shape that fit against him like a matching puzzle piece. There was an audible click in her ears that assured her she was exactly where she was meant to be.

Then he fit his mouth to hers as though he'd been kissing her for weeks, months, centuries. His aftershave filled her nostrils, and the lights went out as she closed her eyes. His hand brushed her naked shoulder, and she parted her lips under the pressure of his.

His taste filled her senses.

It was nothing like any kiss she'd ever experienced.

Time stopped. There was only heat and wildfire. Devastation as he tore down her defenses and slowly rebuilt her, altering her so she was utterly his. So she wanted to be his.

As surrender shuddered through her, the officiant said something. Her father chuckled.

Oh no.

Axel's breath hissed in. He reluctantly lifted his head.

Joy resisted losing the taste of him, clinging to his lips with her own, then didn't know where to look so she stared at his tie. She must be glowing red as a traffic light at having put on such a display. At having revealed how reluctant she was to stop.

Axel's gruff voice abraded her ears. "Let's finalize this. We have a plane to catch."

Joy had never been so aroused from lengthy lovemaking, never mind a single kiss. She was utterly destroyed, but despite Axel's relentless push for the marriage, he seemed content to take his time over brunch with her father, his assistant and the two strangers who had performed their nuptials. In fact, he put up with a number of probing questions from her father before they left for the airport.

Thanks to Paul's quavering inquisition, Joy now knew her husband was an only child. His father had passed when he was young, he enjoyed skiing in winter when he had time, he traveled for work, not pleasure and had no pets. He missed the challenge of being directly involved in the design process with complex projects but took great satisfaction in overseeing multiple international projects and making top-level decisions.

He had politely asked about her father's lifetime working in mortgage and loans, then reassured him that he would bring Joy back for the big move to California. The unit Paul had chosen would be ready by the time Carrie's baby was due. In the meantime, a private nurse had been hired along with a daily housekeeper. An assistant would also help Paul downsize and pack.

Joy's marriage erased her father's financial worries and ensured his day-to-day life would be much more comfortable. Leaving him was still hard. And even though her stress over providing for him was lifted, Joy was more anxious than ever.

Marry in haste, repent at leisure, her lawyer, LaShonda, had said with a glower of warning. Joy had picked LaShonda from the three she'd interviewed because LaShonda had been the only one to ask if she was out of her damn fool mind. Then she had proceeded to wield her red pen like a rapier on the prenuptial contract, building in enough protections to raise Axel's eyebrows.

"If she wasn't working for you, I'd hire her myself," he'd drawled, then signed off on all the changes.

Before they left for their flight, they changed into travel clothes. Axel now wore dark green trousers with a black sweater that hugged the musculature of his shoulders and chest. He pushed his sleeves up to expose his forearms.

Why that detail seemed so important, Joy wasn't sure, but she found herself staring at his strong, flat wrists and the light hairs decorating the fading tan on his skin. She kept thinking of their kiss. Kept thinking, *I'm his now.*

That knowledge sank deeper and deeper into her psyche, swirling in her belly as they climbed aboard a private jet. This was her very last chance to reverse this mad decision she'd made, but within minutes, her opportunity to escape had folded and disappeared with the landing gear.

They were in a luxurious cabin with deep swivel chairs facing a dining table while Heskel retreated to a smaller cabin in the back.

"Do the pods back there recline into beds?" Joy asked curiously, stifling a yawn.

Axel glanced up from reading something on his tablet. "Are you tired?"

It was only the middle of the afternoon, but she admitted, "I was too nervous to sleep last night." Or the night before. "Do you think they'd mind if I used one?"

"You're not sleeping in the staff cabin," he said disdainfully. "We have a stateroom." He rose and moved to open a door she had thought led to a bathroom.

She followed out of curiosity.

Like the rest of the jet, the stateroom was furnished in a style of minimalist luxury. The bed was huge, made up with a snowy white duvet and overstuffed pillows. Big windows revealed an indigo sky over a layer of pink clouds as they headed into dusk. At the foot of the bed was a flat-screen television recessed into a bulkhead of cupboards and drawers.

Axel acted as though a private jet was a perfectly normal way to travel, but all of this was completely surreal. Especially the part where she was married to him.

What if he's dangerous? David had asked in predictable big-brother protectiveness. Joy had tried to play it off that this was a normal thing to do, that this was merely a business deal.

Nothing about their kiss had felt normal or businesslike, though. Kisses were acts of affection. Sometimes they warmed her up for a more intimate encounter, but they never sent bolts of lightning crackling through her nerve endings, igniting a desire in the pit of her belly that lingered for hours afterward.

"Do you want something to sleep in? Or dare I hope you sleep naked?" Axel leaned his shoulder against the bulkhead. He let his gaze stray unabashedly and possessively down the formfitting yoga pants and loose pullover she wore.

"I—" her heart lurched "—don't think I'm ready for that."

His gaze rose to hers, full of lazy amusement. "Sleeping naked?"

"With you," she confirmed in a quavering voice. It felt like a lie. She definitely didn't feel tired anymore.

"The bed is big enough we won't bump into each other unless we want to." His tone altered, becoming more businesslike. He straightened off the wall. "I expect Otto to attack the validity of our marriage. He may even report us to immigration. If he doesn't recognize our union, he won't have to honor the contract. For that reason, we'll share a bedroom."

"And I should lie back and think of Vorstoben?" she asked with acerbic irony.

"I do enjoy that bite of yours." He ambled toward her. "You're going to need it."

Her stomach flip-flopped with nerves as he neared,

but she stood her ground and bared her teeth, clacking them in a threatening snap.

"Not with me," he chided. "You're tired. I respect that. I won't touch you until you say you want me to. But do you? Want me to touch you?"

He was so close, she had to tip her head back. Her neck felt weak as a broken flower stem, helpless to the crushing weight of his sex appeal. She felt the trace of his gaze against her lips as though it was his fingertip. His tongue.

She licked away the tickling sensation and saw the flash in his gaze.

"You have to say yes, Meine Schönste." His maddening voice seduced her. "Say you want me to kiss you again. Küss mich bitte," he prompted in a voice that was wickedly compelling. Mesmerizing.

"Küss mich bitte," she repeated, trying the words, but also because she did want him to kiss her again.

It's only a kiss, she thought before he cupped the side of her face and sealed his mouth over hers.

Immediately, they were back to that wedding kiss, but this time there was no one to stop them. This time, he rocked his mouth to part her lips and his tongue invaded her mouth. It should have been too blatant too soon, but she hadn't stopped thinking about this. Wanting it. She brushed her tongue against his and delicately sucked.

A feral noise resounded in his throat, one that pleased her into almost smiling. Then his hand bracketed her waist, ran to caress her hip, then back to her rib cage and across her lower back.

Swirls of pleasure unraveled like yarn in her abdomen. His touch felt so good.

She moaned into his mouth and slid her arms up to his shoulders, angling her head in offering, twisting her body to invite the delicious stroke of his hands. *Touch me,* she telegraphed as he set her ablaze.

His mouth ravaged hers while his hands claimed the rest of her—spine and shoulders and the cheeks of her ass. His palms slid to draw drugging circles on her backside, then clenched her buttocks, making her lift onto her toes in erotic delight.

"Say mehr bitte," he commanded in a rasp against her ear before his busy mouth moved to her neck. "More," he translated. "Ask me for more."

She couldn't think, could only tremble while his lips sent shivers into her throat and delightful tingles into her breasts. Her nipples stung, and her arms clung, and she was arching to feel the thickness behind his fly against her mound.

"What do you want, Joy?" His head came up. His tongue flicked at the corner of her mouth. Then his wide palm pushed into the notch of her thighs, claiming her swollen mound with such deliberate, possessive pressure, lightning shot through her.

A ragged groan left her.

"You want this?"

No one had ever made her feel so good with so little effort. She had always had to self-serve if she wanted an orgasm, but she was already so aroused, so delirious with lust, she said, "Yes. More. Bitte."

His kiss drew her back into the velvet darkness, and his hand pressed more firmly. Rocked. Deliberate and unhurried.

She was dimly aware of fisting her hands into his pullover and arching to ensure his touch was exactly in the perfect spot. Exactly the right amount of pressure.

Breaking from his smothering kiss, she gasped urgently, "Don't stop. Please don't stop." She was taut as a bow, supported by the strength of his arm across her back. *This is paradise*, she thought. This was how it was supposed to feel. This was the kind of sex she'd been promised by books and movies and whispers and giggles over wine.

"What do you need?" He kept up the delicious rubbing, but added a tiny bit more pressure. A fraction more friction. Some low, filthy words about how he wanted his tongue *right here...*

His touch pressed the center of her pleasure, and she broke, crying out as contractions struck her middle, collapsing her knees.

He kept his hand there, practically holding her up while she clung and shook and panted. Her pulse had its home in his palm, ringing through her body while she turned her face against his shoulder and saw the door was still open to the lounge.

"Anyone could have seen us," she said in horror, lurching away from him on shaking legs.

"We're newlyweds. No will come looking for us," he said dryly. "But I'll leave you. Sleep well."

She stared with bewilderment at the door he closed behind him.

A hand on her shoulder woke her.

Joy snapped her eyes open, completely disoriented to

find herself in bed, the room lights dim, the white noise of the jet's engines filling her ears.

"I didn't mean to startle you." Axel sat on the edge of the mattress and soothingly stroked his hand down her bare arm. It sent titillating tingles through her bloodstream that were deeply unwelcome when her defenses were still below zero. "We'll be landing soon."

She sat up, then regretted it. It put her too close him. She inched away. "I didn't think I would sleep so hard."

"No?" Was he laughing at her? Jerk. It had actually taken her a long time to fall asleep while she stressed out over marrying a stranger, one who could take her apart without any effort whatsoever, then walk away.

Eventually, she had stripped down to the T-back bra and boy short underwear she'd been wearing beneath her yoga clothes. It was more than she wore onstage, but she felt very naked wearing so little right now. Sensitive. And deeply aware of him on a sexual level.

An image of him flattening her to the mattress sprang into her head. It should have been accompanied by alarm, but the fantasy sent a golden heat spiraling through her, making her breasts feel heavy and their tips tight. An ache hummed to life between her thighs, carnal and wet. Receptive. Her skin called out to him, begging for his touch.

Embarrassed and confused by this potent, relentless attraction, she moved farther toward the middle of the bed. She glanced over to see an indent in the other pillow and a discarded blanket atop the wrinkled covers.

"You slept here?" That made her feel even more vulnerable.

And resistible. Unwanted, even. It was a lesson in how uneven this relationship truly was. She would have to guard herself more carefully against him.

"For a few hours," he replied. His eyelids were heavy, his mouth relaxed. He was watching her in a way that said, *I know what you're feeling*.

Mortification became a hot coal in the pit of her stomach while a guiltier heat throbbed in the notch of her thighs.

"Would you like to join me in the shower?" His voice was so low, she felt it more than heard it. It resounded inside her, making her heart thud.

"No." It should have come out firm and strong, but it was thin and high. Strained but also defiant as she took back a little of the control she'd surrendered earlier.

His fingers twitched into a loose fist where his hand rested on his thigh, then relaxed. He rose abruptly, making her stomach swoop. "Wise. We'd be on the tarmac for hours."

"You really take a lot for granted, don't you?"

He only looked down at her with those flame-blue eyes. "Do I?"

He walked into what she'd already seen was a spacious lavatory, especially by airplane standards. It didn't have a bathtub, but the shower could easily accommodate two.

Don't think of it.

As the door closed behind him, her exhale burst out of her. She dropped her forehead onto her knees, wanting to run, but where? She was on an airplane a mile over the ocean. Or Britain, maybe, since they were getting close to landing.

Close to meeting her father.

She had so many mixed feelings about all of this, but now she had to confront her worries over meeting Otto.

Was he really as callous as Axel had implied? She'd read the contract he'd had Axel sign and practically memorized the letter from her birth mother. It did seem dodgy that Otto had known about her for three years but had only reached out to her a week ago, but maybe Axel was misrepresenting things. She'd only heard his side of it, and he'd blinded her with his generosity toward her and her adoptive father.

She knew Axel's support wasn't coming from the goodness of his heart. He was using her to one-up Otto.

Leading up to the wedding, she had told herself she didn't mind because she was using him, too. She wanted better care for Paul. She wanted her family together in California. She wanted to dance.

And she wanted to meet her birth father.

What if Otto was angry with her, though?

Over the years, she'd talked to other adoptees and had had several in-depth conversations with her sister-in-law, Carrie, who was a family therapist. Joy would have sworn she had long ago made her peace with being relinquished by her birth mother. Wendy and Paul had given her a very stable, privileged, loving upbringing. Yes, there were times Joy had felt like an outsider in their family, but that wasn't because of anything they had done. It was all in her own head.

Then Wendy had died, and Joy had felt so adrift she'd reached out to the agency, seeking a connection with her first mother only to learn that she was gone, too. They had refused to provide more than her name. That loss had hurt in a way Joy hadn't expected.

That was when she had realized that she harbored a deep, hidden sense of rejection along with a heavy weight of obligation toward her adoptive family. They would never want her to feel that way, but it was there all the same.

As for her birth father, he'd remained a mystery. She had considered doing one of those ancestry tests, but learning Lorena was dead had been such a kick in the stomach, she hadn't had the courage to look for her father. She'd also had all that drama with Todd messing with her head, then moved home. She had been struggling to survive ever since.

Now here was Axel claiming he would protect her from Otto.

Maybe, deep down, she had latched onto that promise because she was so fearful of another rejection. Maybe she was still looking for a connection beyond her adoptive family, one that didn't come with tangled emotions of gratitude and indebtedness.

And maybe she had married Axel because she knew she wouldn't see him again otherwise. She had been enthralled with him from her first glimpse of him. She didn't want to be, but she was.

She had also thought this intense attraction was mutual, but he really seemed to be able to turn it on and off at will, which was painfully lowering.

The bathroom door opened. Axel emerged in a towel, bringing a spicy fragrance of aftershave with him, sending a punch of sensuality into her middle.

She was still sitting in the bed and pushed her legs toward the edge of the mattress. "You're quick."

"I can be," he said laconically. "When the occasion demands." He pressed a section of wall to open a closet, revealing a handful of suits.

She stared at his naked back. Had that been a *sex* joke?

She threw off the covers, starting to rise, but he turned to show her a small gift bag. He ambled toward her with his towel sitting low and loose and precarious across his hips.

"What—" She had to clear her dry throat as she was confronted by his stacked abs and the sprinkle of hair that arrowed down from his navel. She fixed her gaze on the black bag with its gold embossing and satin ribbons for handles. It matched the shop where they'd bought the wedding rings. "What is it?"

"A thank-you," he said. "A sweetener, maybe."

She hesitantly took it and peered into the bag, drawing out the black octagonal velvet box. Not another ring? She pried it open.

"Oh my God." It was a ring. Two pear-shaped stones, an emerald and a yellow sapphire, sat at angles to each other on a coiled platinum band caked with small round diamonds. "Why...?" She looked up, up, up at him.

"I saw it when we were picking the wedding rings." He rolled his smooth shoulder. "It reminded me of the way you wrap yourself around the pole."

A sweetener. Do you want to join me in the shower?

"And how do you expect me to thank you?" she asked with a thrum of disenchantment, offering it back. "Wrap myself around your pole?"

"You already said no to that," he reminded pithily. "So I took care of myself."

The ball of heat that exploded within her was impossible to hide, especially because *he* knew she was picturing him erupting into his own soapy hand.

"I can also be quiet when the occasion demands," he said with a mocking smirk. "But don't feel you need to be. Shower's all yours."

"Oh shut up." As if she would do *that*, knowing he was out here listening! She dropped the ring and the box onto the rumpled blankets and stood.

He caught her arm before she'd taken a step.

She flung a glare of temper at him, as if she wasn't looking for an excuse to wrestle with him across those tangled covers. As if his burnished skin didn't make her mouth water and she wasn't dying to know how the point of his nipple would feel against her tongue.

"Wear it to our meeting with Otto." He turned into the jaded executive before her eyes, naked chest and slipping towel notwithstanding. "He'll interpret that you've thanked me appropriately and know you're firmly on my side. That you're mine."

His crude, possessive words crashed through her, inciting a flutter of intrigue but toppling her belief that they were anywhere near equal in this sea of sexual attraction that was drowning her.

"I really am just a pawn to you, aren't I?" She shook off his grip and locked herself in the bathroom.

CHAPTER SEVEN

NOT A PAWN. A queen. One with enormous power to run the board. That was why he'd captured her.

Axel hadn't amassed this much wealth and power so he could be treated as a pawn, though. And that was what Otto wanted to do. Axel's solitary focus right now was performing this checkmate on Otto.

Or should be. He was having a hard time thinking beyond the way his wife had shattered under his touch a few hours ago. And how sensual and flustered she'd looked when he'd had to wake her.

He hadn't meant to let their kiss flare out of control, but she had smelled so damned feminine and sweet. Her body was both strong and softly curved. He had felt her shiver and heard her breath catch, and the most primal part of him had taken over.

He had nearly lost himself behind his zipped fly. Everything in him had wanted to pick her up and set her wilted body on the bed. To continue what they had started.

She could unravel him as easily as he had her, he had realized while she'd been trembling and panting in reaction. That was sobering enough to make him walk away if only to prove he could. The last thing he wanted was to be under her sexual spell if Otto managed to turn her against him.

He was reminded he had higher priorities than consummating his marriage when he picked up a panicked message from Vorstoben's CFO a few minutes later. Mira was making good on her threats to pull the properties she'd allowed to be used as collateral. Refinancing was necessary. And urgent.

A second message from Otto demanded Axel come see him the moment he landed, to discuss their plan of action.

Axel's plan was to oust Otto and negotiate with Mira. He would have to hit the ground running if he wanted to keep the financial impact of her anger from cratering the whole organization, but he was confident he could do it.

The stateroom door opened, and Joy came into the main cabin.

Wrestling his libido back into its crate was next to impossible, however, when she looked so delectable. She wore a fitted, cream-colored dress that closed with two gold buttons beneath her left breast. It hugged her curves to her knees and dipped modestly in the front to reveal the beaded lace that decorated the top of her slip. Her muscled calves made his mouth water.

"Do I look okay?" she asked with a self-conscious brush of her hand against her hip. "I bought it when I got my wedding gown." She smoothed her hands down her backside as she sat in the chair across from him.

He'd blamed their prickly banter in the stateroom on

sexual frustration and lack of sleep, but it struck him that she was nervous about meeting Otto.

"You look perfect." She wore enough makeup to hide her jet lag and her hair was gathered into one of those braided patterns that mysteriously consumed its own tail. She looked chic and feminine. Aloof, sophisticated.

Yet there was an underlying vulnerability that pierced through his thick armor.

"Don't let his opinion matter to you," he asserted. "I've seen that movie. It ends poorly."

"I can't help how I feel." She defensively crossed her legs and looked to the blur of gray morning clouds they ducked beneath to land.

A protest rose in him, but he couldn't allow softer feelings like pity and protectiveness impact him too deeply. He needed to be completely impervious as he faced down the man who had double-crossed him.

They deplaned for his car and, a short while later, arrived at the Vorstoben building amid the usual morning bustle.

Axel was greeted with respectful nods. Security guards hurried to open gates and press buttons for elevators, glancing curiously at her, but Heskel had already registered their approved guest. No one asked her to identify herself.

The way Joy twisted her new ring while they rode the elevator had Axel capturing her cold fingers in his, refusing to allow any show of weakness. Her nails cut against his skin as they moved through the top floor of white and chrome decor, spiking the aggression simmering within him.

Outside Otto's office, they were greeted by a pair of assistants who scrambled to open the doors for him and Joy to walk through.

Otto was at his wide desk, the city showcased through the floor-to-ceiling windows behind him. It was a deliberate arrangement. Otto liked to be backlit and make people squint.

His features were sagging with age, but his golden-brown gaze sharpened as he sat back. He didn't smile, only stared at Joy in a way that picked her apart.

"Joy, Otto Braun." Axel heard her swallow. "Joy Youngston," he provided to Otto. "Your daughter."

"Enja." Otto rose to come around to the front of his desk. "Umberto said you'd done the test." He gave her a calculated study. "You look like your mother."

"Axel showed me a photo of her." Joy's expression flickered with a hesitant, unsteady smile. "I have so many questions about her. And you. It's nice to meet you." She tried to take her hand from Axel's so she could move forward and offer it to Otto.

Axel didn't allow it. He kept her by his side in the middle of the room.

Otto's attention swept down to their locked hands, then snapped up to meet Axel's gaze. Questioning. Narrowing with suspicion.

Axel smiled with raw satisfaction. Grim triumph.

"You insisted I marry her." He lifted her hand and turned it, flashing the ring he'd given her on the plane before twisting the other way to reveal the plain band on his own finger.

"You were supposed to come to me first," Otto snarled at Joy.

Axel felt the jolt of shock travel through her. Her features contorted with injury.

"Don't take this out on her." Axel stepped forward, reflexively angling to shield her while drawing their linked hands behind his back so his bulk was between them. "This is the deal you struck." Axel had no compromise in him. "I've held up my side. Now honor yours."

"Like hell." Otto shifted so he had a line of sight on Joy. "He's taking advantage of you. He married you because he thinks he can get my money. My company. I was saving it for you."

This was why Axel had wanted her vow to him before she met Otto. The old man was already trying to manipulate the situation to favor himself. That infuriated Axel, but it didn't surprise him.

"She's seen the contract," he told Otto. "She knows exactly what you expected from your biological daughter."

"I wouldn't have forced you to marry him. Is that what he told you? That you had to marry him? If he bullied you, this can be annulled," Otto said.

Over my dead body, was Axel's very primitive and disturbing thought.

"Come. Let's talk." Otto waved at the sofa, cannily trying to read Joy, trying to find the inroad to turn her against Axel.

She looked to the sofa, confused. Tempted. "Why did you want to meet me?" Whatever optimism had been in her face had faded into a frown of anxious wariness.

"You're my daughter. Why wouldn't I want to meet you?"

"But why did you set up that contract before you had?" she asked. Her nails were cutting into Axel's hand again.

"That was business," Otto dismissed with a patronizing wave that said, *Don't trouble your pretty little head*.

"He's known about you for three years," Axel reminded her with brutal honesty. "He didn't reach out until I threatened to leave. He wants to use you to keep me in line. She's no longer available for that." Axel turned spitefully toward Otto. "She's already my wife."

Otto muttered a word in German that was very foul.

Joy didn't need a translator to know what he had called her. Her breath cut in as though he'd struck her.

"Watch your mouth," Axel warned in a lethal tone.

She looked to Axel with eyes full of disillusionment. Blame. *How could you bring me here for this?* Tears gathered in her eyes, and she flexed her fingers, trying to extricate them.

He held on, unable to regret bringing her here even though she might never forgive him for it. "You're already bleeding cash reserves," he reminded Otto. "Step away from the company, and Mira will have no reason to continue her attacks on it."

"It's my company," Otto insisted with a rabid shake of his jowls. "I decide what happens here."

"You signed a contract. Honor it."

"You questioned the validity of that contract yourself," Otto threw at him. "We'll see what the courts say."

"Lawyers it is, then," Axel said darkly. "But make no

mistake. I will get this company if I have to join forces with Mira and take it, brick by brick."

Joy didn't pay attention to where Axel took her.

She was aware of feeling cold until the weight of his suit jacket was draped over her shoulders. She heard him say something in biting words she couldn't understand. Her vision was blurred, and there was a scorch in her throat that stretched into her chest, making even her shoulders ache with the effort to hold back her tears.

In those first seconds of meeting Otto, her hopes had been sky-high. Surely Axel was wrong about him. Surely her birth father—who had asked her to come meet him—would be glad to see her. Surely, he was eager to know everything about her, the way she wanted to know everything about him.

Seeing him had given her a disconcerting sense of recognition, one that disarmed her because she thought she ought to feel a sense of belonging from that vague familiarity.

But as she had looked for an answering interest in his expression, her soft, jumbled emotions had collided with instinctual dislike.

It wasn't Axel's warnings poisoning her opinion. Otto had radiated coldness. He had kept a distance between them and made her bristle with the way he looked at her. His gaze hadn't had the lecherous quality of the men at the club, but it had been a cousin to it. He had called her by her birth name and mentally calculated her intrinsic worth based on her off-the-rack dress and how likely he was to get what he wanted from her. He'd regarded her as an object, not a person. She'd felt it.

Despite all the things she'd told herself for years, all the *just curious* justifications she'd made in the last forty-eight hours, she had come here yearning for a sense of homecoming. She had wanted him to open his arms to her. She had wanted to feel wanted. She had wanted to be missed.

Instead, she'd been disdained. Scorned. She was suffering a depth of disappointment that threatened to drown her. She was in such pain, she didn't want Axel to touch her, but she needed his help drawing her out of the car. The strength of his arm across her back was necessary as he guided her stiff, frozen body into a new building.

He brought her into a silent apartment. She had the sense of being on the top floor because the ceilings were high above exposed rafters. Angled windows poured light onto the combined kitchen, dining and living area. There was a terrace, but she only stood at the closed double doors that gave access to it, staring blindly at concrete tiles and empty flower boxes.

"You're upset," he said grimly. "You have a right to be. His behavior was appalling."

"His?" she choked and swung around to confront him.

"He was always going to be exactly as you met him today," he asserted as he yanked off his satin tie. It was such a dark blue, it was almost black. "You would have come here whether we married or not. Wouldn't you? You wanted to meet him."

She clenched her teeth, refusing to admit that because it sat too close to the hidden longings inside herself. No, she had never expected anyone to show up and save her, but she had wanted them to want to. She had wanted someone to say, *I would have kept you if I could.*

She had wanted Otto to say, *If I had known about you, I would have found you sooner.* She had wanted him to say there was a good reason—a really good one—that he had waited to reach out to her.

Otto had let her down so crushingly, she felt sick with it. She wanted that not to matter, but it did.

"He would have tried to use you, one way or another," Axel continued brutally. "Against me, against Mira. Whatever served him." He opened his collar button with an impatient twist, then his cuffs so he could roll them back. "He would have tried to use your family troubles to keep you in line. By marrying me, you took control and made that impossible. He can't hurt you now."

"He already has," she blurted, voice catching raggedly. "I want to go home." She wrenched at the rings he'd give her, struggling because her fingers had swollen overnight. "I'll find a way to pay you back f-for everything—"

"Joy, stop it." His hands tried to capture hers, and she knocked him away. "You're angry with him so you're trying to run away from me," he said sternly. "Stay and fight."

"I don't want to fight," she cried. "I was happy as I was."

"Like hell you were," he snapped back. "You were already in a fight, and you were losing."

"So what?" She stepped in close to confront him. "I didn't ask you to fix it for me! I sure as hell didn't ask you to bring me to *this*." She was starting to break apart, emotions rising to burn hot against the backs of her eyes, elevating the pitch in her voice. "I just wanted my father to be okay. And you took advantage of that." She poked him in the chest. "You knew how desperate I was, and you used it."

"Yes," he agreed flatly. "But I'm on your side."

"You're on *your* side." She clenched her eyes tight. Tears solved nothing, and it felt so weak to weep, especially when she had done this to herself. She had agreed to come here. She had married him, deluding herself into thinking this would work in her favor.

"We're on the same side," Axel insisted.

"How? I can't trust you. How could I?" She snapped her eyes open.

"I told you exactly what was going to happen." His unflinching stare hammered that home to her. "I didn't lie about any of it."

That was why this was worse than what had happened with Todd. Axel might not have lied the way Todd had, but she had still fooled herself into believing things would be different. She was devastated by her own gullibility. She was hurting and exhausted, far from home and very alone. That was what she was facing as she stared at him. She was starkly alone. She always would be. It was terrifying.

"Can I trust you?" The bite in his voice sent a chill across her skin, raising the hairs on the back of her neck. "Because you promised me a year."

She'd seen how he reacted to people who broke their promises. And backing out now would mean more than dissolving this marriage. She would have to find a way to cover her father's bills again. Beg the neighbor to help with his care. It was so daunting, hot tears rose afresh behind her eyes.

Axel had her cornered, and he knew it.

A phone rang, startling her so badly she jumped.

"It's the doorman telling me my lawyer is here." He moved to a cordless phone on an end table and spoke briefly before clicking it off and setting it aside. "What's it going to be, Joy? I need to know whether you're staying so I know how to direct him."

He sounded completely removed from the outcome. He didn't care whether she stayed, not beyond how it affected his plans, only that she be clear in which way she would jump.

"I don't have a choice, do I?" she said in a garbled voice. Then, because she needed to collect herself and wash off her makeup before she cried it down her cheeks, she asked, "Where are my things? I want to change."

"Upstairs," he said remotely.

The elevator dinged a warning that it was about to open, so she hurried to trot up them.

CHAPTER EIGHT

Joy had never felt more powerless in her life. Axel had taken more than her body into his hands in the last twenty-four hours. Her finances and her family's welfare were also in his control. Most painful of all, she'd let him make one of her most deeply hidden dreams come true, and it had turned into a nightmare.

Not that it was his fault that Otto was utterly disinterested in her. She hadn't seen anything more than calculation in the older man's gaze even before he'd known she and Axel were married. No curiosity or sentimentality. Her initial thought had been, *This is why she didn't put his name on my birth certificate.*

In fact, Joy had to wonder if her birth mother had been protecting herself by not telling Otto about her pregnancy. Lorena would have been tied to Otto forever if she had kept Joy and told him about her.

Axel was also correct in saying that if he hadn't interfered, she would have come here to meet Otto. And, yes, she would have wound up exactly this disappointed.

By marrying me, you took control...

It didn't feel that way at all! She felt overwhelmed and raw and homesick, but it was too early to even call her father to let him know she'd arrived safely. There was nothing he could do to help her, anyway. She texted that she had landed safely and sent another to her brother. David was in Guam, but he typically only replied when he was off duty. It wasn't unusual for days to pass before she heard back from him.

At this rate, David was only going to say *I told you so*, and she deserved it.

This was the deal she had struck, however. Had she really thought there would be no cost to her?

She snorted at herself, realizing she had to shake off whatever expectations she'd had and deal with what was. She had to accept that she had landed herself into this situation and figure out how to take charge from here.

She started by pulling herself together physically. She changed into her favorite jeans and a snug striped top, then brushed out her hair and washed her face, reapplying just enough makeup to hide the distress around her eyes.

Then, because she hadn't had more than a cup of coffee since leaving Chicago, she made her way downstairs, planning to raid the refrigerator.

Heskel was here, setting the table for two. "Frau Severin," he greeted with a polite smile. "Are you hungry?"

"Starving," she admitted, then glanced around warily, bracing herself for the aggressive energy that her husband gave off with a single look.

Can I trust you? You promised me a year.

She had, and it was really landing on her what a daunting promise that was.

"Where's Axel?" she asked.

"In with Gerard." He nodded at a closed door. "He

said you should eat while it's hot. He'll join you as soon as he can."

He removed a covered dish from an insulated bag and set out a plate for her. The crepes were still steaming and had a bluish-purple compote drizzled across them.

Her stomach panged, and her mouth began to water.

"Please," Heskel invited, holding her chair. "Would you like coffee? Juice? A mimosa?" He set out a basket of pastries and a pretty parfait of yogurt, berries and muesli.

"I'd love a coffee, thank you."

While she was trying to eat with more grace than a lion pouncing on a kill, Heskel set a cappuccino above her plate. A swimming swan was drawn into its foam.

"That's beautiful." She was charmed. "Were you a barista in a past life?"

"I was." He glanced over the table with a critical eye. "What else can I do for you? Unpack?" He glanced to the loft.

"You could call me Joy," she suggested. "And keep me company." She was feeling very friendless at the moment, trying to imagine how she could make this work.

"When we're not in public, of course. Joy," he conceded with an amiable nod. "I have the same arrangement with Axel."

"Have you worked for him long?"

He hesitated, then said, "Four years."

"Was that too personal? I didn't mean to be."

"No," he said on a slight laugh. "It was a trick question. Until an hour ago, I was employed by Vorstoben, but also as his assistant, so my answer stands."

"Did they fire you because of this?" She used the tip

of her knife to motion between herself and the closed door, appalled to have any part in his losing his job. "I'm so sorry."

"Don't be." He waved off her concern. "They offered me a raise to stay and assist Herr Braun in Axel's absence. I'm privy to the status of all the ongoing projects and have a good rapport with contacts inside and outside the company. I prefer to work for Axel, so I declined."

"Oh." She considered that level of loyalty as she chewed a bite of cheese-stuffed crepe. "I'm not asking what they offered you, but I'm curious how much a good salary for an EA at a company like Vorstoben is?"

"In US dollars?" He looked upward as he performed mental math. "They offered me around one hundred fifty?"

"Thousand?" She dropped her fork so it clattered against her plate, nearly choking on her bite of food. She forced herself to swallow, then gasped, "And you turned that down?"

He brought her a glass of water, biting back a grin of amusement.

"Axel and I have a standing agreement that he will better any offer I receive, including and especially from Vorstoben. It was in my best interest to hear them out, so I did. When they'd gone as high as they were likely to go, I texted him the amount. He asked me to pick up breakfast on my way over."

"Oh my God. I mean, good for you, but oh my God." She cleared her throat with another sip of water, boggled. All of the money Axel had thrown at her and her family now seemed like pocket change. Apparently, it was. For him.

She was starting to think she'd sold her own loyalty at far too low a rate.

"The truth is, I'd work for him for a tenth of that," Heskel confided. "He helped my husband and me out of a very tight spot a few years ago."

"You're married? You seem young for that."

"So do you," he said with an ironic tilt of his mouth. "Klaus and I weren't married yet, but we were living together when he was in a terrible car crash."

"How awful. He survived, though?"

"Yes. And he's mostly recovered, but he still has some pain if he sits or stands too long. That's prevented him from taking full-time work again. He's an industrial engineer. Axel had just recruited him to Vorstoben when it happened. It was a good job, so we thought it was the right time to buy a home together. Nothing extravagant, but when he couldn't work, things became difficult."

"Don't you have social programs here?"

"We do. And they gave him a package that covered lost wages, but it was a reduced rate. Even so, I was only working part-time around finishing my degree. I had to quit both to care for Klaus. We were looking at having to sell our new home and move to something smaller. It was a lot to deal with, but Axel heard what had happened and checked in with me. He wound up covering the shortfall on our mortgage." Heskel shook his head and looked away, dampness in his eyes. "I asked him how I could repay him. He said to work for him when I was ready. I'm resourceful and have good communication skills, but my background is marketing in the food industry." He shrugged, seeming perplexed. "He said he wanted someone he could trust. He can. With your marriage, I extend my loyalty to you." He turned a magnanimous palm toward her.

"Unless my needs conflict with his," she surmised with a tense smile.

"How do you foresee that happening?" He canted his head in curiosity.

"Well, you haven't given me back my passport. I take that to mean you won't help me leave if I decide I want to go home."

"I always hold the travel documents when I fly with him." He moved to a leather messenger bag and brought her passport to her. "I'm sorry if you felt I was restricting you. That's not the case at all." He set the passport on the table.

She checked that it was hers, feeling churlish when she saw that it was.

"If you ask me to book your flight or make arrangements for you," Heskel continued, "I will feel compelled to tell him what I'm doing. But you have your phone and credit cards. You can do that yourself if you want to. He expects confidentiality from me, not blind obedience or illegal confinement."

"I sound paranoid, don't I? My ex gaslit me constantly. And everything you just told me seems so…" She couldn't call it out of character for Axel since she didn't really know him. All he'd shown her was a ruthless will to get Otto's company, no matter what it cost in dollars to him or heartache to her. "My impression is that he's very practical and single-minded and only helps people if it serves his own agenda."

He couldn't have known whether he was buying Heskel's loyalty, though. That suggested a decency she hadn't credited him with.

"He's an engineer," Heskel said with amused affection. "I say that because I'm married to one. Their priorities are efficiency and finding a way to get the result they want in a consistent way. But I don't want to gossip about him. I want to carry out the tasks he has assigned to me. He asked me to support you in looking for a dance academy. A friend of a friend owns a studio here. He studied at the Royal Ballet in London. May I set up a meeting for you? I'm sure he could give you some guidance on how best to pursue your goals."

Her jaw almost unhinged and fell onto the floor. "When did Axel ask you to do that?"

"During one of our meetings in Chicago. It took me some time to get to it, what with the wedding and everything else."

"I'm not complaining." They'd only landed a few hours ago. Her suspicious mind had leaped to thinking Axel was trying to make up with her after their argument, but this wasn't a bribe or an apology. He was only holding up his end of the deal they'd struck. That was a little deflating, but also reminded her that if she was going to stay in this marriage, she might as well get what *she* had been promised. "I would love to meet your friend. Thank you."

The idea of speaking with a professional dancer lightened her mood considerably.

"I'll call now to set that up." Heskel stepped away.

The door to the office opened a moment later. Axel came out with a man who could have been thirty or fifty. He had more salt than pepper in his closely shorn hair, but he didn't have a wrinkle on his dark brown complexion.

"Joy. My lawyer, Gerard."

"Hello." She found a smile and rose to move to Axel's side. "It's nice to meet you."

"My wife, Joy." There was a note of something in his voice—pride, maybe? Whatever it was, it felt at odds with the anxiety she felt in being his wife, leaving her flustered and blushing.

The way he casually set his hand on her lower back sent unexpected warmth shooting into her limbs, but she did her best to play her part, shaking hands with Gerard.

He warmly invited them to dine with him and his wife as soon as possible.

"I'd love to meet her, thank you," Joy said sincerely.

"I'll have my assistant set it up, but please excuse me." Gerard nodded wryly at Axel. "I have a mountain of work ahead of me."

They walked him to the door. The second it closed behind him, Joy stepped away from Axel's touch.

His brows went up in question.

She only hurried back to the table, thinking that if she was staying and playing the part of his wife, she needed a better grasp of what he expected of her. She might react to him, but he seemed very take-it-or-leave-it about her.

Heskel was setting out Axel's plate while wearing his earpiece, speaking German to someone. His tone held a distinct, *I have to go* flavor as he hurried to end his call with, "Bis später."

"Klaus?" Axel guessed as he held Joy's chair. "Take a few days at home with him since I won't be working. We'll be in Paris." He nodded at Joy as he took his seat.

"Paris? We just got here." This man refused to let her get her feet under her, didn't he?

"You need clothes. Our wedding announcement has gone out?" He glanced at Heskel, who looked up from texting to nod a confirmation. "Invitations will start coming in. I instructed Gerard to sue Otto for breach of contract. He agreed that Otto is likely to attack our marriage, so we need to show people it's real."

But it's not. She didn't say it aloud, but Axel's gaze was waiting to snag her own when she flashed a look at him. He held the eye contact in an implacable way that had her throat flexing in reaction.

By marrying me, you took control...

She absolutely needed to do that, but how?

"My work phone was confiscated before I left the building," Heskel said. "I'm sure people are trying to reach you. Would you like me to do anything about that?"

"No. Let Otto answer for my absence. If he doesn't see the light and retire before we return from Paris, I will open my own firm. Vorstoben's clients will turn to me out of frustration. If anyone reaches you in the next few days," he added as he dug into his breakfast, "let them know I'll be in touch after I return from my honeymoon."

Joy choked on her bite of parfait. *Honeymoon?*

As a courtesy to Mira, Axel hadn't taken a lover in two years. Celibacy hadn't always been comfortable, but sex wasn't something he had ever felt he needed.

Not like he did today.

And when it came to sex, he was all for edging. To a point. Now that he knew how responsive Joy was, how she melted and sounded when she shattered, he wanted more. Needed more.

"He will attack your marriage any way he can," Gerard had warned him during their meeting. "How strong is it?"

"We've known each other three days. What do you think?" Axel had asked dryly.

Otto's potential attack wasn't why Axel wanted to bind Joy to him physically, though. Nor was it his lengthy dry spell, though that was definitely a factor. They were married. Why shouldn't they have sex if they both wanted it?

This particular shade of want, however, was biting and primitive and disturbing.

For that reason, he kept trying to put a lid on it. He didn't want to want her this hard. It felt too much like those times he'd wanted other things he couldn't have, like parents who took care of him or a hot meal.

Maybe if she wasn't so frosted by how things had gone with Otto, things would be different, but he couldn't change what had happened and wouldn't if he could. At least she had stayed and would continue this pantomime they were calling a marriage.

He didn't want it to be pantomime, though. He wanted the reality of touching her. Covering her. Claiming her.

Don't, he ordered himself, but his ears were ringing with the sound of her footsteps as she explored their suite in the Paris hotel.

His eyes refused to look away from her, only noting

very absently the backdrop of tasteful creams and dull bronze, white sculptures and pink floral arrangements.

She wore boots with her jeans, giving her strolling steps a swagger that entranced him. She paused in the rounded nook of windows that offered a view of the Eiffel Tower shining golden against the purple clouds of fading dusk.

They had both fallen asleep on the plane from Berlin. It was too early to go for dinner. What else were they going to do right now?

"Heskel told me how you helped him and his husband. Do you mind if I ask why?"

He lifted his brows. Heskel wasn't usually so forthcoming.

"I knew Klaus from school. We'd kept in touch, which is how I knew to recruit him. I was working in Hong Kong when his crash happened. It took a few weeks for me to get back here to visit them. When I saw Heskel, I saw myself." He winced at how uncomfortable it made him to refer to his darkest days even in passing. "I recognized how much stress he was under, trying to keep them afloat. It looked a lot like the way you were drowning when we met," he said sardonically.

Her brows came together crossly. "I was fine."

He ignored that blatant lie, saying, "I threw him a life ring because I wished someone had done that for me. You asked me why I continued working for Otto even after I knew what sort of man he was. Because, in many ways, Vorstoben was my life ring. Seeing the way Otto dismissed Klaus without telling me was the beginning of me making plans to leave, though."

"Hmph." She moved past the doors to the balcony, skirting the end of the sofa to the bookshelf. Hardback copies of French classics stood next to framed black-and-white photos of Paris streets. She peered into the bedroom.

"Only one." She sent him a cool look. "I'm sure you think I'm very casual about sex, given my line of work."

"I didn't say that."

"You didn't have to."

"I don't care how you made ends meet, Joy. I was poor for the first half of my life. If I'd had a skill like yours, I would have used it, so I don't judge how you leaned into yours."

"What did you have?" she asked with a curious tilt of her head. "To rise to a life like this? Besides a job at Vorstoben?"

"Hunger." Literally. He tucked his hands in his trouser pockets and leaned on one of the square mirrored columns. "A ferocious desire for security and control over my future. Single-mindedness." Desperation, at times. "I was fifteen when I worked on a hotel like this." He glanced around. "An iconic building getting an upgrade. The furniture they threw out was nicer than anything I'd ever seen. I stole a chair from the dumpster and took it home to my mother. She still has it. She loves it. I remember promising myself every morning, when I arrived on the jobsite, that one day I would stay in places like this and not think twice about the cost."

"Is this the first time you've thought about the cost today?" she asked with a twist of humor on her lips.

"I haven't at all. Heskel booked it." He shrugged.

"I've been pinching pennies for so long, I can't imagine that sort of confidence." She touched the bouquet on the bookcase, realized the flowers were real and cupped a bloom, bending to inhale its fragrance.

He let his gaze trace the line of her back, the roundness of her ass, the beautiful length of her legs.

She glanced up and caught him, not that he was hiding his interest.

A light blush stole into her cheeks. She dropped her gaze to the flowers, toying with the petals. "I keep wondering if you're still in love with her."

"Who? Mira? No," he dismissed firmly.

She angled her head, studying him from the corner of her eye. "That sounds like you don't even like her. But you were going to marry her?"

"She's fine." He heard how lukewarm that sounded and curled his lip at himself. "We're friends. Soldiers in the same infantry, maybe. I've never wanted love in my relationships, and she knew that." It was probably a good idea to make that clear to Joy as well.

"Why not?" She blinked in a way that asked, *Who doesn't want love?*

"It weighs too much. Fills you with obligation and gives others leverage over you."

"Like the way you exploited my love for my father to pressure me into marrying you?"

"Yes."

Her brow flinched, but that wasn't new information. She seemed to mentally brush it aside. "You were marrying Mira for the company? Same as me?"

"Yes. We've known each other for years. I've dined

with her and Otto enough to say we're more than acquaintances. Once we were engaged, we went to a lot of functions together, but..." Could it even be called dating? "Honestly, *that* was more of a paid escort situation. Without the sex," he added with self-deprecation.

"You didn't have sex with her?" She tucked her chin, skeptical.

"Now who's making snap judgments about promiscuity?"

"It's not promiscuous to have sex within a committed relationship. You were engaged for a long time." She was still wearing a look of incredulity. "It's a reasonable assumption that you would have slept with her."

"I barely kissed her." It seemed important to him that she know that, but he didn't dwell on why. "I wasn't attracted to her, and I was under the impression her interest was directed elsewhere."

"But you were going to marry her anyway?"

"It was a business arrangement."

"Isn't that what this is?" She pointed between them. "Would you have had sex with her if you actually married her?"

"Probably not," he said truthfully. "We had planned to divorce after a year, same as this. I didn't expect our engagement to last so long, but it turns out you don't actually die if you don't have sex. It just feels like you will."

"But you want to have sex with me?" That was not an invitation. It was barely a question. Her arms were folded, her shoulders stiff. Unreceptive.

"I do," he said, keeping a tight rein on his libido.

"Why? Because you're horny after going without for

so long? And I'm convenient?" Her jaw lifted to a belligerent angle, but her eyes were full of watchful, vulnerable shadows.

His desire for her was far more personal than that, not that he was comfortable admitting it. "I want to have sex with you because we react to each other. Whether this level of desire is convenient is very much up for debate." His guts were tangled in knots of want and his own resistance, not wanting to be pulled this hard. "What exactly is the reason for this line of questioning? Are you angry that I called this a honeymoon? We don't have to have sex if you don't want to." It hurt at a cell-deep level to say that. His libido howled and fought being shoved into its crate.

"I don't think I'd sell that lie very convincingly after what happened on the plane, would I?" She looked past him to the windows, cheeks bright pink, brow gathered in disgruntlement. "That's why I thought you must think I'm someone who falls into bed with anyone who flips a bill at me."

"I don't." The sharp claws that were clenched around his vitals shifted, taking a piercing grip into his groin. "This is a conversation we should have, though, so tell me what you're thinking."

"That I wish I was the sort of person who did sleep around," she admitted with a tight press of her lips. "I've only slept with one man, and I attached way too much emotion to it. That didn't serve me at all."

One?

"The man you lived with?" How could he instantly feel so much resentment toward a stranger? A single, solitary man with whom she regretted becoming too attached. "What happened?"

"Short answer? I let him use me." She sent him a faint, ironic smile as she let that penetrate. "Not in the way you're doing it. At least you're open about how you want to use me." She looked to the floor, brow heavy with self-recrimination. "I didn't see what he was doing for a long time."

"Why not?"

"I don't know. It was gradual. Like, he forgot his wallet so I would buy lunch. Then it was bigger items. A jacket he wanted. He would promise to pay me back, but when I asked him about it, he'd point out that his parents hadn't set up a college fund for him the way mine had. Somehow, he made me feel petty for having more and wanting to be paid back. It was a rough time. I had just lost Mom and learned that Lorena was dead. I wanted someone in my life I could count on."

"And he took advantage of that." He really did hate this other man.

"He said that living together would be cheaper, and it was. For him," she said on a snort. "I paid the rent. He swore that it would all wash out as soon as he got through dental school and started working. I don't know if it was a line or if he really believed it, but I believed it. So, when he couldn't finish an assignment, I did it for him. When his tuition was due, I paid it. And when it came down to choosing between my dance aspirations or working full-time to pay the bills, I picked the wrong horse. I thought he was my person, though. That we were in love. You support the people you love, right?"

This was the problem with love. It became a liability. It might be nice to have, but it did not pay the bills.

"He told you he loved you? To keep you there?" It was exactly the guilt trip that tightened his skin and made him prickly with ire.

She nodded, expression flexing in shame.

"I will never lie to you like that, Joy. If you need love in order to have sex, then I understand. I'll leave you alone." And he would throw himself off the balcony because the next year was going to *hurt*.

She searched his gaze until he began to feel it like too much sun on his face. "I don't think I could sell that lie very well, either," she said with a break in her voice and looked away.

The tug in his groin was visceral. Dear God, she was going to kill him, dancing around the pole between yes and no.

"That's one of the reasons I thought I could go through with this marriage." She trailed her fingertips along the edge of the desk. "I confused sex and love before, but I don't love you. How could I?"

Ouch. He didn't know why that stung, but it did.

"We've only known each other a few days," she clarified, brow pulled in consternation. "I thought that meant I was safe from you yanking me around by my emotions. I didn't expect we'd jump straight into a physical relationship. I didn't know you would make me want one."

He bit back a groan. His ears stung, he was straining so hard to catch every word spilling from her lips.

"You already hold all the financial cards. Now you want this from me, too?"

"Most of my relationships are transactional. I admit that," he said grittily. "But you already gave me leverage with Otto that I wouldn't otherwise have. As long as you stay married to me and play your part, you don't owe me a damned thing. I'm not trying to extract *more* from you."

"No?" Her brows went up.

"No. If we have sex, it's because we want each other."

"Do you want me, though?"

"You doubt it?" No one had ever said anything so astounding to him.

"You're very hot and cold." Her mouth softened into a pout. "'I can wait,'" she quoted mockingly. "You had no trouble walking away from me on the plane."

"Do you think that was easy?" he asked with a rasp in his throat. "I only meant to kiss you, and you damn near turned me inside out. One of us has to keep a few brain cells working. Otherwise, we're liable to burn this place to the ground."

"Really?" Her mouth tilted with shy amusement, and her lashes flared. He suspected if he stood closer, he would have seen her pupils explode.

The air became fully charged with the electricity they'd both been trying to ignore. Sparks of heat began to catch in him like hungry flames on dry grass, threatening to surge forward in an uncontrolled sweep of licking fire.

"Really," he said in a voice that had dropped into the pit of his chest. "If you want more orgasms like that one on the plane, get the hell into that bedroom and take off your clothes." He pointed.

Oh, she hated being told what to do. It was very exciting, the way she stood taller and lifted her chin to that haughty angle.

Wordlessly, in the way of an old aristocrat dropping a glove, she pushed her jacket off her shoulders and let it fall to the floor. She set her boot on the edge of the chair and lowered the zip. The boot hit the floor, then the other. She held his gaze as she peeled her shirt up and off, revealing a pale purple bra with translucent arcs across the tops of the cups. Her jeans relaxed across her hips as she released the button and fly. With a wiggle, she dropped them, leaving her yellow thong in place.

When she reached to open the front closure on her bra, he let his beast off its leash.

CHAPTER NINE

"I'M NOT IN the bedroom!" Joy gasped as Axel pounced on her.

She pushed her hand against his shoulder, not sure what had possessed her to provoke him like this. A desire to see if she could get a reaction out of him? Gain the upper hand in some way? No chance of that!

"You chose the bed, Honigbiene. Lie on it." He tipped her, pressing her to the lacquered top of the Louis Quinze replica, shoving the small lamp out of the way so it fell with a dull thud to the floor.

This was what she had wanted, she realized, as he filled his hands with her. The way he claimed her made her feel wanted.

Even so, the hard desktop had her arching in protest. "It's cold!"

"You'll warm it." He used his weight and leverage and the cup of his hand on her breast to keep her in place while he buried his lips in her throat.

Her skin felt so sensitive, the desktop was almost painful, as was the friction of his trousers between her thighs.

"Axel," she gasped, cradling his head in her hands.

"Too fast?" He lifted his head and kissed her, but his

wicked hands were on her breasts, teasing her nipples until she twisted beneath him, unable to bear the tendrils of heat sparking from her breasts to her loins. "This is all I've thought about since the moment I laid eyes on you."

She sobbed out a noise of acquiescence, pleased with that confession, but she was bombarded by so many sensations she didn't know how to cope with it all. The brush of his tongue swept against hers. The faint stubble on his chin rasped her skin. The knit of his pullover slid against her chest and stomach and beneath her hands as she clutched at the flexing muscles of his back, sending her plunging straight back into the eroticism of their encounter on the plane.

She jerked her face to the side, trying to catch her breath.

He moved his seductive lips to her ear, wafting a wicked chuckle against her cheek. "Open your eyes, Honigbiene." He licked beneath her ear, over to her throat.

She dragged her heavy eyelids open and turned her head to look up at him.

"No. There." He turned her face to the side again. "That woman has been driving me insane."

They were reflected in the mirror mounted on the pillar. She was essentially naked with one breast exposed, nipple standing high, beaded with arousal. The other was hidden, possessed by his hand, the tip soon captured by the hot suction of his mouth.

She cried out as dangerous, thrilling sensations shot into her pelvis.

As though he knew exactly how fiercely she yearned for his touch there, his hand swept down her waist and hip and thigh, caressing behind her leg until she lifted it to his waist, allowing his clever fingers to follow the crevice to where her thong was damp with arousal.

She groaned and wriggled again, but he was too strong to evade. Too enticing to resist. He mercilessly sucked her nipple while tantalizing her needy core.

A gruff curse left him. "I want to eat you up." He straightened and easily lifted her hips, pulling her underwear free so she was naked to his gaze.

Before she could close her thighs, he was hooking her legs over his shoulders while dropping to his knees at the edge of the desk.

"I don't—" Her voice was lost in a groan as he used his thumb to caress and part her folds.

"Let me have this," he said with a catch of intense craving in his voice. "You don't know how badly I need this."

She had never responded to oral, but she'd never responded to being felt up before, either, and he'd nearly killed her with an over-the-pants fondling.

Her flesh remembered exactly how adept he was. She was already achy and needy and soft. Shaking in nervous tension and painful anticipation.

It was beyond blatant, the way he was looking at her. Talking to her in a soothing way as if he had some kind of pity in him when he clearly had none. Not the way he was toying and avoiding, then spooling out the expectation in her with a soft "hah" of his hot breath against her most sensitive flesh.

"Axel, please," she groaned, somehow remembering, "Bitte."

He rewarded her with a slow, benevolent lick.

She could have screamed, it was such a tortuous relief. She turned her head, but her vision was blurred with lust. Her hand was trying to form a fist in his hair, but the strands were too short. She could only catch the silky tufts between the fingers of one hand while she gripped the edge of the desk above her head with the other. She braced one foot on the shelf in the wall and the other dangled off the edge of the desk.

It was the height of debauchery. She had completely abandoned any sense of propriety. Of self. In the mirror, she watched the rock of his head as he lewdly pleasured her and it turned her on. All of this turned her on so much, she could only groan in ragged ecstasy.

He teased her with the addition of a finger, then a second, and found a rhythm that paired his penetration with the sweep of his tongue. She knew she was making the most lascivious noises, filling the room with them as she dug her foot onto the shelf and lifted her hips into his pleasuring.

Maybe she was even saying "please" again. Over and over because the coil of sexual tension in her was so tight she thought she would explode from it.

Then she detonated, and it was as powerful as before. More. It went on and on because he did not let up. Her powerful climax rolled into a fresh, intense arousal that made her sob in frustration. How could it be so good and not enough?

Gently he withdrew his touch and left a wet bite against the inside of her thigh. She instinctively tried to pull away, but she was utterly wrecked. She had the vague thought that she ought to close her legs or tell him she wanted a real bed. Something. But she was too weak to move, and she'd fallen too deeply into the well of lust to do anything but watch as he peeled off his sweater.

He withdrew a condom from his trouser pocket before he opened his fly and dropped his pants enough to bare his ass and his erection.

Since when did she think *that* organ was beautiful? But that most brutally masculine part of him, turgid and aggressive, made her ache with yearning. She watched him apply the condom and had to swallow an agony of need.

"Say yes, Schatz. I will die if I can't have you right now."

"Yes," she gasped and started to crook her knee, but he drew her legs up so her ankles were on his shoulders.

His cheeks were flushed, his expression intense as he guided his thick length to the sultry flesh that was still tingling with sensitivity. Still pulsing with greed.

As his hardness began to fill her, he hugged her legs, keeping her still for the careful pulse of his hips. The shallow, testing strokes sent delicious spikes of heat through her whole body, making her shake and groan.

"Good?"

"So good." She bit her lip and clutched the edge of the desk again, holding herself still for a deeper thrust that told them both she was more than ready.

"Now, my pretty wife." He caressed all around where he was penetrating her, awakening her into a fresh flood of heat and yearning. "I want every last person in Paris to hear you scream my name when you come."

They did.

* * *

I confused sex and love before.

Had it been sex like that? Because Axel could see how it rewired the brain.

That was a disturbing thought, mostly because he didn't care to think of her with her ex, giving that other man even a fraction of her extraordinary passion.

His animosity wasn't jealousy, precisely. It was a deeper, more justified contempt toward someone who had taken advantage of her when she'd been struggling with grief, tricking her into financially supporting him.

Was he any better, though? Axel wasn't bankrupting her, he reminded himself. Quite the opposite. And he wasn't lying to her about how he felt, either.

He still found himself brooding on whether he was treating her fairly. What more could she want, though?

I don't love you. How could I?

And why in hell would he feel a compulsion to give her more than he already had?

Because that sex had been outstanding.

After defiling the desk, he'd carried her in here to tear up the bed. She was magnificent. Strong and flexible, and she had a stamina and sexual appetite to match his own. Her sensuality ran deep enough to bury him. She wasn't afraid to push back. Or demand.

Ringing cries of ecstasy from her had been as satisfying as his own incredible orgasms. It had been spectacular. Euphoric. He wanted to envelop her and hide her from the world. *Mine.* But he also wanted to worship her. Celebrate her.

He reminded himself that he was breaking a long fast.

The physical relief and sexual triumph from that alone was profound. But he instinctually knew sex wouldn't have been this intense with any other woman. What was it about Joy? Purely chemistry? Or was he drunk on the way their marriage had given him the upper hand with Otto?

That was a prickly thought, but there was some truth to it. Certain exultant emotions were riveted into this act that he didn't care to examine right now, because his battle with Otto wasn't finished. Axel was merely enjoying a moment of respite while he gathered his forces for his next move.

Joy was a key member of his assault. That was why Axel was so eager to spoil her, he reasoned. He wanted this marriage to appear watertight.

Was *that* transactional? Manipulative? Perhaps. But throughout his life he'd been taught that he could get what he wanted if he provided what others needed, whether that was food, labor, technical skill or other resources. That was how he'd climbed the ladder at Vorstoben. He'd met Otto's need for a leader with business acumen and management skills. In return, he'd gained the secure, comfortable lifestyle he wanted. When his desire had shifted to wanting autonomy, Otto had appeared to offer that as well, while needing Axel to marry his daughter.

Axel was a transactional person, but woe betide the person who tried to cheat him once they'd agreed on a price. He would get Vorstoben or an equivalent repayment of the time he'd put into it. That was nonnegotiable.

Not that marrying Joy felt like a high price right now.

He sent a look of consternation across to her angelic face, relaxed in sleep.

No, he knew what was really bothering him. She had accused him of being hot and cold, and he was. He preferred his walls and autonomy, but he wasn't a heartless bastard. He couldn't completely shut down on her after she'd given herself so generously to him.

This was why he'd been okay with marrying Mira—he didn't like bumpy emotions or the ability to bruise someone's feelings. He didn't like that hurting Joy was now a conduit to harming himself. She had become as much a liability as asset.

He needed distance from those barbed thoughts and her.

He left the bed. As he snapped his briefs into place, she drew in a sharp breath and blinked, brushing her hair off her face.

"What time is it?" she asked with soft urgency, picking up her head.

"Six thirty."

"I need to call Dad." She dropped her head back onto the pillow, eyes fluttering shut again while her brow flexed. "I texted when we landed in Berlin and told him I'd call once he was up. He must be worried."

"Do you want me to find your phone?"

"No. I'll, um—" She sat up, pulling the sheet up under her arms as she did. "Is there a robe in the closet?"

"Really? I've seen everything you have under there." And had run his hands or lips over every square centimeter, in case she'd forgotten.

"*I* decide how much skin I reveal and to whom," she said with a clash of her gaze into his.

She was putting her own defenses into place.

His logical, civilized brain said, *Fair*, but the possessive animal in him bristled and said, *Actually, that's mine. No one else will ever see that much of you again.*

What a hypocritical reaction.

Dismayed with himself, he moved to the closet, then held plush robe ready for her, rolling his eyes to the ceiling with great sarcasm. "Should I order room service? Or would you rather go out?"

She *tsked* at the way he held the robe and stood to shrug into it, yanking it from his grip as she closed it across her front and tied the belt. "Whatever you prefer."

"What I prefer..." He caught his fingers under the cinch of her belt. "Is to eat in, drink wine in the tub, then climb back into that bed for another round or three. Lights off, if you prefer not to show me what you have."

"I'm allowed to have boundaries." Her chin came up in shaky dignity. "Don't make fun of me for it."

"I wasn't joking about any of that."

She sniffed, but some of her tension dissipated when she said, "Fine." Her brows gave a haughty little jump. "To all of it. But the lights can stay on. Wear a blindfold." She started to brush past him.

He snagged his arm around her waist, amused and, yes, titillated. "Really?"

"I don't know!" she said with exasperation. "Maybe it will give me the upper hand for once."

As if she needed it.

Tightening his arm, he brought her hip into the twitching flesh at his groin and clasped a fistful of her hair with his other hand, slowly dragging her head back so her hands clutched at his arm and her lips parted on a startled inhale.

He kissed those soft lips, taking his time with it, savoring the way she softened and leaned into him.

When she danced the tip of her tongue against his, when she was breathless and her lashes seemed too heavy for her eyelids to lift and her lowered gaze was hazy with desire, he drew back and released her.

"Say hello to your dad for me." Before outrage could take hold in her eyes, he added, "I need to order dinner. And a scarf."

"Springtime in Paris!" her sister-in-law had exclaimed, very taken with their honeymoon location.

Joy promised to send photos but suspected the city was overhyped. That is, until she and Axel were actually walking through the streets where trees and flowers were coming into bloom.

"I feel like I'm in a movie," she said, stopping on one of the pedestrian bridges over the Seine to snap photos of the river, swollen and glugging slowly beneath them. It was flanked by buildings freshly washed by last night's rain. Everything smelled fresh and gleamed in the morning sun, inciting a sense of possibility in her while breaking her eyes at how pretty it all was.

"Including the Hollywood makeover," she added when she turned the camera for a selfie and was freshly startled by her polished appearance.

Axel had booked her into the hotel salon first thing, then bought her a new outfit from its posh boutique before they left. She wore a pair of wide-legged designer jeans with a snug crop top and a black satin jacket.

"Do you want a trophy wife or something?" she asked him now.

"I have one," he said laconically as he leaned his forearms on the rail.

She captured his possessive look in the frame as she clicked.

"I knew we'd be photographed once the news got out." He straightened to draw her into his arms, pulling her hips into a light collision with his own, one that sent delicious sensations sloshing through her belly.

The press release had been very brief, stating only that Axel Severin had married American Joy Youngston on the heels of his broken engagement to Mira Braun.

"Won't people assume I'm the reason you two broke up?" she asked, trying and failing to be as casually unaffected by their closeness as he seemed.

"Probably." He brushed at the bangs she'd had trimmed into her hair after the color was adjusted to a more natural honey and molasses tone. "That's why we must appear smitten."

This was all an act for him, but it was nearly impossible for her to think when he touched her.

"What if, um, they find out that Otto is my father?" She dropped her voice to a near whisper. "Isn't it PR 101 to stay ahead of something like that?"

"The only way they'd learn it is a leak from Otto or Mira. Otto isn't likely to acknowledge you until he has to. He would have to admit to having an affair while his wife was pregnant. It then opens the question of whether you have any rights to his fortune. I don't think Mira will say anything, either. She hasn't made public yet that she's not Otto's daughter, probably because she's exploring her own legal options. We're at an impasse. Which suits me. It allows you and I to establish ourselves as a couple before Otto takes any shots at us."

"Is that why you're kissing me right now? Are you paying to have us photographed?" She tipped her head back and narrowed her eyes in suspicion.

"No. But I might have if I'd thought to do it. My mind has been on other things." He was obscenely handsome when one corner of his mouth kicked up that way.

He'd relaxed significantly from the first time she'd seen him. She didn't have to wonder why. After getting a little drunk over dinner last night, they'd bathed together, spending a lot of time tenderly washing their dirtiest parts. Afterward, they made love again, slept hard, then barely got through breakfast before they were at it again.

If he had suggested going back to the hotel right now, she would have gone. She was smitten. Or infatuated, at least. Sexually.

And disconcerted because, as much as he seemed beguiled by their sexual connection, she didn't think he was anywhere close to as enthralled with her as she was with him.

"Didn't you say I had an appointment?" she reminded him, trying to gather some of those brain cells he said they ought to keep hold of.

"You do." He finished walking her over the bridge to a designer's showroom.

The next few days were spent browsing exclusive boutiques, picking up everything from dance shoes to sunglasses. Everything. The lingerie purchase alone would have bought her a new car. A nice one.

Between shopping excursions, Axel wined and dined her at street cafés and high-end restaurants. They went out in the evening to art galleries and visited a nightclub and watched a musical production.

He seduced her constantly. He set his hand on her leg while they watched models parade their fashions. He kissed her nape when he seated her in a restaurant. There'd been a particularly erotic and clandestine grope in a darkened alcove when they were walking back to their hotel one evening, one that he ended while she was still tense and whimpering with need.

"If you can't be quiet, I have to stop," he scolded in a way that suggested he was denying her on purpose. "Otherwise, we'll be arrested."

She had thought Todd's manipulation of her emotions had been bad. She was completely at the mercy of Axel's whims. Even when she was anointing him with her mouth, trying to make him break, he was fully in charge of their play.

He cradled her jaw and the back of her head, thrusting with slow, hypnotic precision, saying, "Touch yourself while you do this. I want to come together. I'll tell you when."

She did. And it was so hot, she nearly crumpled to the floor afterward.

This was exactly what a honeymoon should be, she supposed, but on their last night, she pointed out, "I thought this was supposed to be a time when spouses got to know each other, but I don't know much more about you than when I met you."

They were in one of the small dining rooms of a converted four-hundred-year-old residence. The high ceilings wore decorative gilded plaster. Intricate tapestries covered the walls, and intimate light glowed from wall sconces and dripped from crystal chandeliers.

The staff had greeted Axel by name and welcomed her warmly, not giving them menus and bringing champagne without being asked.

"What do you want to know?" he asked, seeming to withdraw several degrees.

That was something she'd become very familiar with.

"I don't know," she mused.

She had learned a few incidental things. He didn't care for seafood and rarely had more than one or two glasses of alcohol. He didn't need much sleep. Twice, she woke to find him out of bed in the night, working. He had a villa on a Greek island, a vineyard in Portugal, a pied-à-terre in London and a unit in a Singapore building that he had helped design, getting in on the ground floor so to speak.

"I guess I'm curious about your childhood. What was it like?"

"Impoverished," he said with a twist of his lips. "Is that not obvious?"

"No, I mean, you told me that's why you were ambitious and why you wanted to live like this." She waved at the amuse-bouche. It was a single bite of puff pastry that turned out to be cheese. It melted in her mouth and made her next sip of champagne explode with flavor on her tongue. "But what were your parents like?"

"Young. Too young," he added with a dismayed curl of his lip. "They were both born in East Germany. When the wall fell, my mother's family moved to Berlin for work. She was thirteen at the time. My father was sixteen and left his family in Leipzig, also looking for work. After a few years, my mother's parents went back to Dresden. By then, she had a job in a café and was finished with school, so she stayed. She and my father went on a few dates and..." He motioned at himself.

"She was eighteen? Nineteen?"

"She turned eighteen two days before she went into labor."

"Oh. That is young. Especially when you don't have family nearby. Your grandparents weren't supportive?"

"They weren't in a position to help. Reunification was a difficult time. There was a lot of unemployment, prices went up. Everything my parents had known growing up had changed. They married because it seemed like the right thing to do, but they didn't have much between them beyond hormones and a baby they weren't ready to parent."

Everything in her went still, concerned about what that meant. Afraid to ask.

"They weren't abusive. Not intentionally." He spoke conversationally but seemed to have retreated a million miles into himself. "They tried. And argued because they failed. My father did whatever he had to, to keep us fed. Stole. Sold drugs. My mother took them, trying to cope. She's sober now, but after my father was killed, that was a dark time."

"Axel, I'm so sorry." She put out a hand on the table, but he ignored it, face looking carved from granite.

After a moment, feeling spurned, she slowly pulled her hand back into her lap. "Were you ever put into care?"

"A few times. I didn't like it." He grimaced in distaste. "It was too regimented. I'd been raising myself since I could walk. I didn't trust their charity and didn't want to answer to anyone. I didn't want their pity. I hated their judgment." He picked up his wineglass.

Joy had experienced something similar. Not often, but she knew the quizzical look that searched for the flaw that explained why her birth parents had failed to look after her.

"But you still see your mother?" she asked gently. "How is your relationship with her now?"

"She lives in a house I bought for her in Dresden. We talk every week or so. I told her about you and said we'll visit as soon as we can. She tries." His shoulder jerked. "She made amends with me a few years ago, acknowledged her shortcomings and asked me to forgive her. I do. I can see that she was set up to fail, being so young, but..." His brows lowered in dismay. "She wants me to feel the kind of love a child is supposed to have for their parent, and I don't. It's not a grudge. I just learned that it didn't matter if I loved her. Loving someone doesn't mean your needs will be met. All it does is make you feel like you owe them something."

Joy's heart took that like a punch. She wanted to argue that maybe, if his parents had loved each other, things might have been different for all of them.

But maybe they wouldn't have. How could it be proved either way?

"I can't say Otto was a father figure to me. It was never like that, but once he began recognizing my efforts, I was able to leave struggle and instability behind. So I felt some loyalty and obligation. I'm furious with him for tricking me, but much of my anger is with myself. I let myself believe in him when I already knew I'm the only one I can count on."

She had thought she was cynical. The hardness in his expression sent frost creeping through her chest.

"That's why I can't let him get away with cheating me," Axel continued grimly. "There were too many times in the past when I had to accept the insults, the theft, the beating. What I'm after isn't vengeance, Joy. It's justice."

She nodded, understanding, but stunned with hurt over what he didn't spell out—that he would never give up his heart. Not to her or anyone else. And didn't want hers, either.

It's only one year, she thought for the millionth time. And, paradoxically, also thought, *That's not enough.*

CHAPTER TEN

AXEL HADN'T EXPECTED to like being married. In fact, he'd braced for the worst since his parents' marriage had been a strong advertisement for cutting line before things got worse than they needed to be. Plus, after living on his own for so many years, he had developed an appreciation for order and quiet and minimalism.

Joy's things were everywhere, especially when they got back from Paris. They had to convert the spare bedroom into a dressing room to accommodate it all.

Oddly, he liked seeing her clothes next to his in the closet. He liked hearing her talk to her family over the tablet before they went to bed. He liked coming home to someone and eating meals with her, and he liked being out with her.

They'd gone out every night in Paris, but she was visibly nervous the first night he took her to a cocktail party in Berlin. She was worried there would be a language barrier and judgment over their quick marriage.

She charmed everyone they met, of course. She was naturally curious and wry and so attractive in a beaded black cocktail dress, everyone was dazzled to be in her sphere.

The next day she had her first meeting with Heskel's friend, the dance instructor. She was nervous about that, too.

"I'm rusty," she said as she anxiously tried to choose between two leotards that looked identical to him. She was packing a duffel so full, it looked as though she was leaving for a week. "The school I was at was good, but it wasn't the Royal Ballet in London. I want him to be honest, but I don't want him to be too honest, you know? A wrong word from him could kill my dreams."

His hackles went up. "Do you want me to cancel my meeting and go with you?"

"No. I don't want you to see me humiliate myself." Her tone asked him how he dared make such a stupid suggestion.

Heskel arrived then to take her to the studio.

Axel quietly relayed in German that his assistant should ensure zero wrong words were spoken to his wife and was told, "I'm confident he'll be completely professional."

Axel was distracted through his meeting, though, troubled by thoughts that this instructor would deride Joy in some way. He wasn't used to being concerned about someone, not beyond the level of basic decency. His mother had been a source of constant distress when he'd been a child, but this was different. Joy wasn't engaging in risky behavior like drug use. She was worried her feelings would be hurt.

So was he.

Unable to stand it, he cut his meeting short and had

Heskel text him the address so he could catch up with them before she finished.

When he arrived, she was kneeling on the floor in the middle of an otherwise empty dance studio. Her eyes were closed. She wore a black sports bra and pair of matching yoga shorts, but nothing else.

Heskel motioned him to quiet while a recording of a haunting female vocalist began to play.

With slow grace, Joy took hold of her own head, drawing it down so her body followed. She flowed into a snakelike move and kicked one leg up straight. That turned into a cartwheel that put her on her feet. After quickly tiptoeing across the room, she crumpled into a handful of bends and swooning movements that synced with the music. The emotion in the song poured from her limbs and her face and the butterfly lightness of her leaps. The yearning of the vocals chased her around the room, making him catch his breath and clench his fist in an agony of longing as she stood on one foot and reached toward him, the distance seeming to be a thousand miles.

Axel was spellbound until the final moment when she returned to the center of the room and did a slow spin that pulled her down, down, down until she was only a ball on the floor.

What else could he do but throw his hands together in claps that reverberated around the big, empty room?

"My employer," Heskel said ruefully when the instructor, a man in his sixties with white hair and a lean, tall posture, shot them a frown.

"My husband," Joy said as she popped up from the floor, scolding, "You distracted me." She hurried toward the instructor and listened attentively as he critiqued her performance.

"Look after yourself when you get home," the instructor reminded her as he brought her to where Axel and Heskel were waiting.

"I will. Thank you so much." She was damp with sweat, but her smile was pure radiance.

I gave her this, Axel thought, and found himself despising her ex yet again for taking dance away from her.

"It went well?" he asked when they were walking to the car. "No humiliation?"

"Oh, he didn't pull a single punch," she said with a sheepish laugh. "But in terms of a master class, that single opportunity to have his one-on-one attention for an hour was beyond anything I could ever hope for. Thank you." She hugged his arm.

He slipped his arm around her, pleased to see her showing so much exuberance. "Will he take you on as a student? What happens next?"

"Flatterer. I'm not that good! No." She tucked herself more fully under his arm as they walked. "His focus is ballet, anyway. He said my foundation skills are solid, that I have nice musicality, but that I need to work on my physical strength. He could tell I've been developing certain muscles and not others, which affects my alignment and some of my transitions. He liked that I learn fast and know how to correct myself, but I need more height in my leaps. He's going to put me in touch with a student choreographer who is putting something together for a festival in May. It's a shoestring budget, but they're holding auditions soon. He said if I can get in with them, the training and networking will help me find my track."

She was still in high spirits the next evening when they met Gerard and his wife at a restaurant. Axel could hardly take his eyes off how dazzlingly pretty Joy was as she relayed her excitement about the dance opportunity and traded misadventures with Gerard's wife around the other couple's children and Joy's toddler nephew.

"I miss him so much," she confessed wistfully.

I can give you that, too, Axel thought abstractedly, then frowned because children had never been on his radar. With his upbringing? No. He had always thought to spare a child whatever baggage he would bring to parenting.

Joy glanced at him and must have seen his consternation. Her smile faltered.

"I'll visit the powder room while we're waiting on dessert," she said with a strained smile.

Gerard's wife accompanied her, and Gerard took advantage of having Axel alone to catch him up on his legal position with Otto.

"As we expected, Otto is questioning the veracity of your marriage," Gerard said. "He's claiming to protect Joy's interest. What if he gifts you the company and your marriage dissolves?"

"It won't." The words came out more forcefully than Axel intended, grunted out by the inner Neanderthal who was having the best sex of his life with the woman he'd dragged into his cave.

"He's leaning into the 'married for a year' stipulation," Gerard added.

"He doesn't have a year," Axel derided. "He's scrambling for investment funding to replace what Mira has yanked. Now that she's working with Rocco DeStefano and tying up Rocco's resources, the timing has never been better for me to start my own firm. I can poach from both of them. Tell Otto that his refusal to honor the marriage contract nullifies my noncompete clause. I will act accordingly."

Not that he had been waiting on anyone's permission to start his own firm. He'd already put Heskel on finding office space and staffing it.

When they returned home, he was still turning over the longing in Joy's voice when she had spoken of her nephew.

"Do you want children?" he asked her.

"I—" Her voice turned strangled. She halted in removing her earrings, eyes wide as a deer confronting headlights. "Because of what I said about missing my nephew? I saw you frown when I said that. I wasn't trying to hint that I want a baby. I've actually been meaning to ask you to help me find a doctor so I can use something more reliable than condoms." She turned away to finish removing her jewelry and started on the pins from her hair.

"Meaning you don't want children," he clarified.

"Maybe. Someday. Not now."

"Not with me." That shouldn't be such a kick in the crotch, but it was.

"Not when I'm about to get back into dance. Why? Do you want children?" She turned to face him but contorted her arms, trying to lower the zip on her dress.

He moved across to do it for her, turning her so he could reach. "I wasn't planning to become a father, no. But it crossed my mind tonight that starting a family would go a long way to proving our marriage is more than a piece of paper."

"This is about Otto?" She spun around to face him, affronted. "What are you thinking? That if I continue the man's bloodline, he'll bestow his riches upon me? There is a limit to how far I'll let you use me, Axel. It does not extend to being a vessel that literally carries your 'justice.' I sure as hell won't let you or anyone use my child for anything. Ever." She started to brush past him.

He stopped her.

She knocked his hand off her arm and glared up at him.

"That wasn't what I was suggesting," he ground out. "I thought a family might be something you want. I thought we should talk about it."

"Why would I want to have a baby with you when our marriage has an expiration date?"

"It doesn't," he said in another knee-jerk response. "We can choose whether we end it and when."

"I can't." She took a step back, coming up against the dresser. She grasped the edge of it as though needing the support. Her mouth tightened. She looked trapped. Hurt. "You can decide tomorrow that you don't want Vorstoben and discard me immediately. I can't leave for a year, or there will be unpleasant consequences for my family."

His heart lurched. "Are you saying you want to leave?"

"No." Her brow pleated, and she swallowed. "But don't…" Her voice cracked, and she blinked fast.

"Are you crying? Joy." He hadn't meant to upset her. He reached for her.

"Don't *do* that." She shoved at his chest and stalked past him until she was across the room. "You know you can fry my brain with sex, and that's not fair! What happens when the sex fades? Huh? Do you really see us staying married all our lives? Having a family? That's a real question, Axel. Do you?"

"I don't know." How had this escalated so quickly? "It was just a question."

"Well, stop and think for a minute how loaded that question is for me! My birth mother gave me away. The man who made me, the one you dragged me here to meet, has no interest in a relationship with me. Now you're saying maybe you want to keep me around a little longer, but only maybe? Only if I have a baby that gets you what you want? A baby you don't even want except for what it gets you? Do you hear how cruel that is to say to *me*?"

He snapped his head to the side as though she'd struck him. He felt her sharp words like claws against his cheek. It was an attack he deserved because he hadn't really seen how tender this was for her. She was so good at hiding that particular scar, acting as though her adoptive family had given her all she needed, that he'd forgotten the very real pain of loss and rejection she carried.

"You didn't like it when Otto changed the rules on you," she pointed out shakily.

"I'm not changing the rules." He did want to change the rules, though. He didn't want a hard end date on this marriage. It bothered him to think of her counting down the days. It didn't matter that he understood why she was doing it. He didn't like it. Not at all.

This was the sort of inner turmoil that he had thought to avoid by marrying Mira. They would have easily ghosted through a year of a marriage that was more of a financial partnership, one that wouldn't have caused any ripples in his life. Or his equilibrium.

"I want to give you what you want," he said tightly. Because if he gave her what she wanted, he could have what he was increasingly feeling like he needed: her. "If you wanted children, I wanted you to know I'm open to discussing it. That's all."

She was still standing across the room, arms crossed to hold up the loosened dress that was hanging off her bare shoulders. Her expression was dejected. "I want to be loved, Axel. I want someone to say they want me in their life forever. I want to know that I belong with them for the rest of my life. Can you give me that?"

The sensation that jolted through him could have been the electric charge off a cattle prod. It seared so deeply and painfully within him, it damn near stopped his heart. Because how was he supposed to pay that steep a price? "No."

He heard her breath hiss in as though he'd stabbed her.

"I need to make some calls. I'll join you later." He walked downstairs.

It took Joy a long time to fall asleep.

She hadn't meant to react so strongly to what had actually been a fair question, given they were married and having sex, but it was a very touchy subject for her and not just because of how temporary their relationship was.

The question of children had always been a sharp jab against her skin with a two-pronged fork. She wanted children, and she also wanted a career in dance. It wasn't impossible to have both, but she knew that each was taxing and demanding and required a devoted level of commitment. Both also had a biological clock, one reproductive, the other related to joints and tendons and whatever muscles she might sprain or injure during hours of training and performing.

She still had time to pursue both, but this marriage was eating a year.

It was buying her a year of dance, she reminded herself, which gave her a second chance at the career she'd nearly given up hope on having.

That made Axel asking her to put that aspiration aside and start a family rankle, especially when his reasons had seemed so mercenary.

At the same time, the idea of having Axel's baby was incredibly appealing. One of the reasons she had finally left Todd was the stark realization that she didn't want to have his children.

Axel had all the qualities of strength and health and a well-built nest that would shake awake anyone's ovaries. The ache of yearning went deeper than biology, though, to the part that she had alluded to when she had said she wanted to be loved. She wanted her baby born into love. She wanted *his* love.

Because she was tipping toward that emotion herself.

They were still new, she hurried to remind herself, as

though that would stop this flailing sensation inside her. She couldn't expect declarations of love, especially when that emotion was so very sharp-edged for him.

For Axel, making love didn't *make* love the way it did for her.

That was what was happening to her, though. She grew more enamored and more vulnerable to him by the day.

Which made the fact that he held all the power in terms of ending their relationship all the more pointed. And made his casual suggestion that they could have a baby and stay married tear at the scab on her heart, the one she pretended wasn't there.

She didn't remember falling asleep but woke in the night to an awareness of him beside her.

The distance across the mattress was mere inches, but it felt like an intolerable chasm.

She slid closer, not wanting to wake him but seeking contact. Reassurance at a very basic level.

"Cold?" He was awake and rolled toward her, drawing her into the heat of his body.

He always slept naked while she usually pulled on a short nightie over a soft sleep bra, even if they'd made love. That was what she wore now. She laced her bare legs with his and her lips met the hollow of his shoulder without her even thinking about it.

At the brush of her lips against his skin, the shift of his hand against her back stilled. He was hardening against her stomach and started to draw back.

"I don't want to fight," she whispered into his throat, touching her lips under his jaw. She let her thigh stroke higher against the outside of leg, so her nightgown rode up to her hips.

His breath hissed in, and his hand roamed lower, catching under the lacy hem and pushing it to her waist as he rolled her beneath him. He kissed her. Not rough but hard. Greedy. As though they hadn't seen each other in months. Years. As though he had felt the distance and hated it as much as she did and was determined to close it.

His tongue swept between her lips, telling her what he wanted. *Now*.

There was an urgency in him that tensed all his muscles and made her feel pounced upon, but not in a bad way. There was something exciting in the way he pushed her legs apart with his hard thighs and dragged his mouth to her breast, raking aside lace and cotton as though he'd been waiting too long to feast on her.

He was lighting a fire in her that was more of an explosion, alarming but thrilling.

He wet his finger and pressed it into her, rasping something she didn't catch because her senses were under assault. What she had thought would be tender makeup sex was more of a claiming; one she encouraged by arching herself in offering.

He slid beneath the covers to lick fire into the very core of her, making her twist against the weight of the blanket and the strength in his arms as he hugged her thighs. She couldn't get away and didn't want to, but his caresses were almost too much to bear. Deliberate and demanding.

For the first time, he did not seem to be in control,

though. Not to the extent that he usually was. Each of her responses made him growl or dig his fingers into her thigh muscle or hold her tighter.

As the tension in her belly coiled to exquisite levels, she dug her heel into his back, lifting her hips, seeking the climax he was driving her toward.

He rose and threw off the covers.

She released a loud sob of protest. Agonized denial.

They were both panting. He remembered to put on a condom, which was a nearly intolerable delay, then he dragged a pillow beneath her hips and hooked her legs over his arms.

His first thrust, imperative and wild, pushed a ragged groan from her lips.

He froze. "Too hard?" he asked through gritted teeth. His whole body quivered with strain.

"Too good," she breathed and set her hands against the headboard so his next thrust went even deeper.

"Stay with me," he growled as he quit trying to restrain his power, thrusting with all his strength, fast and ferociously intense as he drove them straight to the peak.

The second her breath hitched and the first flutter of orgasm arrived, he let go, locking his hips to hers while he bucked, joining her cries of pleasure with his own shouts of helpless triumph.

Waves of ecstasy rolled through her for long minutes, keeping both of them in exquisite stasis, pulses fading slowly, slowly, until he sagged all his weight onto her, both of them sweaty and shaking and trying to catch their breath.

She was utterly wrung out, barely able to breathe under

the press of his body, but she twitched in protest when he started to gather himself. "Don't go," she whispered.

His hand clenched in her hair, and his damp lips scraped across her cheek to the corner of her mouth. "I'm not going anywhere, Meine Schönste. Don't you, either."

He had to roll away to remove the condom, but he returned immediately and gathered her close, allowing her to believe what he'd said with her whole, glowing heart.

Until the party on Saturday.

CHAPTER ELEVEN

Joy was gaining confidence with these parties and events, but this charity gala was the fanciest yet, increasing the pressure on her to look her best. To reflect well on Axel.

He was making important connections at these things. He'd been a little more open since their argument the other night, telling her how things were going with Otto—(poorly)—and that he was moving forward with his own firm, courting investors and preparing to take on his first few projects.

That worried her a little. What did he need her for if he had given up on taking over Vorstoben?

He hadn't, he assured her. He had merely accepted that his dealings with Otto would take time so he was pursuing what he'd really wanted all along.

His new venture had lit a fire in him that was exciting to be around. She was already on cloud nine, having made the first cut at the audition process for the festival. Axel's support in her dance aspirations meant the world to her, which increased her desire to do whatever she could to help him get what he wanted.

To that end, she had a professional style her hair and apply her makeup. She broke out the most expensive gown in her closet, one of pale blue satin that made her feel dipped in liquid moonlight. It flowed off one shoulder and down her body, clinging enough to accentuate her curves without being blatant about it.

"You look incredible." He seemed transfixed as he watched her come down the stairs.

"So do you."

He was in a tuxedo, jaw shiny and sharp, ice-blue eyes gleaming with such pride in her, her heart panged with pleasure.

He opened a box and held out a gorgeous bracelet with an aquamarine that closely matched her gown. It was set in ornate filigreed white gold that cuffed her wrist.

"I love it," she said, biting her lip. "But why?" They had made up from their fight.

"I wanted to." He kissed the heel of her palm, then her fingertip.

As he held her gaze, a potent silence fell between them, one that was becoming familiar. It was filled with a helpless sort of energy on her side. His was more difficult to interpret, but she had the suspicion he wanted to be closer to her, he just didn't know how.

"Thank you," she said softly, stepping closer to lightly touch her lips to his, taking care not to stain him with her lipstick. "You really don't have to spoil me, you know."

I'm here, she conveyed, basking in the warm admiration of his half-lidded gaze. She was starting to think she would be here forever. If he would let her.

If he wanted her forever.

Please let him want me forever...

"You're too beautiful," he chided. "We should go, or I'll take you back upstairs."

Perhaps he'd given her the bracelet so she would fit in better, Joy thought when they arrived. She'd never seen so many designer gowns and extravagant jewelry—real diamonds and emeralds and sapphires—outside of watching a red-carpet event on TV.

The wearers were celebrities and high-level politicians, filling her with awe as she recognized them.

Axel seemed comfortable around all of them. Unimpressed, which amused her into relaxing. He introduced her, and most people were polite if not effusively warm. A few were genuinely nice, like the Canadian woman Joy chatted with as they left the powder room.

"I love your bracelet," the woman said. "Can I ask where you found it? I'm looking for something for my sister-in-law's birthday."

"Let me ask Axel."

He was watching for her and approached the moment he saw her looking for him.

The woman introduced herself as Quinn Gould. She was a wholesome-looking redhead with freckles, which wasn't to say she lacked sophistication. Not at all. Her gown was a gold confection that suited her slender figure, and she did *not* look as though she needed advice on where to find good-quality jewelry. She wore emerald earrings and a choker with a square-cut emerald at its center.

"Your husband is Micah Gould?" Axel asked. "We're acquainted. I've been wanting to catch up with him, actually."

"He'll come find me," Quinn assured him. "I ditched

him when he was dragged into a conversation about microelectronics. He knows my eyes glaze over when he talks shop," she confided.

Quinn was in the middle of offering tips on where Joy could take language lessons when an older couple approached the three of them.

Axel introduced them, mentioning the husband ran a company that had been a longtime supplier of steel to Vorstoben. Joy could see him eyeing up the man, trying to discern whether the couple were being polite or if the man's loyalty to Otto was fading.

"I hear you're a dancer," the man said to Joy, cutting though the small talk with the delicacy of a sledgehammer. "Is it true you were stripping in a club when Axel met you?"

Joy heard Quinn's indrawn breath. Maybe it was her own. Adrenaline spiked through her while a heavy blanket of mortification encased her. She wasn't ashamed of dancing at Martini's, but she was sorry her previous line of work had chased her to the other side of the world and was being used to stain Axel's hard-won image.

Especially as he was trying to establish his new company.

"You did not just say that." Axel's voice was positively lethal.

"Am I mistaken?" The man feigned surprise, looking around. "I've heard it from several sources. These things have a way of getting around." He flicked a disdainful look toward Joy as though she was one of those things that got around.

"I think—" Quinn started to say.

Axel stepped right into the man's space and said something in German that had Quinn gasping again.

The other man's wife wore a stony expression, not looking at any of them, but her eyes flared with shock.

"Axel." Joy touched his arm, still feeling stabbed in the lung but not wanting to make this scene any worse than it already was.

"Do not tell me it's fine. It's not," he growled at her.

"No, but I've dealt with this before. Men like him come into the club all time." She let that statement land before adding, "They think I'll put up with being put down, but I don't. You shouldn't, either," she said to the man's wife, startling the other woman into a look of wide-eyed entrapment.

The man's patronizing smirk faded into his own shock.

"I know how hard it is to leave." Joy continued speaking to the wife. "Even when you're being treated poorly. But it's worth it. Reach out to me if you need help. I promise I'll do everything I can to assist you."

"Who the *hell* do you think you are? You—" The man lurched toward her, but Axel fully blocked him, shoving his chest right up against the other man's, pushing him back a step.

"I will rip you in half," Axel assured him.

At that moment, a server came up to ask urgently, "Is there a problem?"

"No." The older man stepped back and grudgingly brushed at his jacket.

"Yes," Joy contradicted, thanking her months in the club for the ease with which the next words rolled off her tongue, firm and assertive. "That man is being insulting and aggressive toward me. He needs to be removed."

Then she walked away, head high. She didn't know where she was going or what happened behind her. She wanted to steal a glass of champagne off a passing tray, but was shaking so badly, she was sure she'd spill it down her front.

She was almost at their table when she realized Axel hadn't come with her. People were glancing at her curiously.

These things have a way of getting around.

More like that man had spread rumors through this room like a virus.

Oh God. Her throat started to ache. She wished the floor would open and swallow her.

"Well, that was some serious badassery." Quinn looped an arm around her. "You and I are going to be *very* good friends. I can tell. Let me introduce you to some of the most sarcastic people I know. You'll love them."

"I—" Joy couldn't help looking back the way she'd come. There was no sign of Axel, which made her heart swerve and dip anxiously.

"I put Micah on him," Quinn said. "He's big enough to hold your man back from the murder he was about to commit. You're welcome for keeping him out of jail."

"I didn't mean to make a scene," Joy said with agony.

"A scene? It was a master class in dealing with ass clowns. 'He's the kind of man who goes into strip clubs and scorns his wife? I'll help you leave him?' That was sniper-level assassination of character. Teach me."

"You're being nice," Joy said, but she found a weak smile as Quinn introduced her to someone from the British embassy. She was acutely aware that Axel still hadn't come after her.

I'll kill him.

Axel was in such a haze of rage, so ready to remove that scumbag himself, he didn't realize Joy had walked away until he heard Quinn say stridently, "Micah! I told Axel you'd find me. He wants to speak with you. I'll go after Joy."

That was when Axel had snapped out of his locked stare to see Joy wasn't here. His whole world screeched to a halt.

"I've got this, big guy." Quinn patted his arm. "You take a beat. And *you*," she advised the piece of crap who'd insulted Joy, "should go save your marriage."

The other man's wife had already walked away as well.

Where was Joy? The ladies' room? Axel looked around. He couldn't spot her.

"What happened?" Micah asked. He was one of the richest men in Europe, running a family conglomerate that had weathered some ethics scandals in his father's time but was now recognized for its green initiatives and commitments to diversity and transparency.

"Gossip." Axel spat the word as though it was the most obscene curse ever uttered. Considering how it had been wielded against Joy, it was.

He pinched the bridge of his nose, sickened that Joy had been attacked. He was livid with himself that he'd put her in the position of becoming fodder for those ugly rumors, then ambushed by such gross behavior.

He glanced for the man who'd insulted Joy, still wanting to close his hand on the man's throat, but that vile filth had wisely dissolved into the crowd. If he had any sense of self-preservation, he had left the party and was on his way out of the country.

"The rumors around you opening your own firm?" Micah said with a frown. "I was hoping that was true. I wanted to talk to you about it."

Axel didn't have much interest in business at the moment, but he exchanged a few terse words with Micah, promising to set up a meeting.

"I need to catch up with my wife and take her home," Axel said.

"If Quinn has her under her wing, they're likely near our table." Micah led him to a small clutch of people who were all laughing except Joy.

She wore a strained smile and clung to a glass of wine, looking brittle enough to break.

"Let's go," Axel said.

She said a stilted good night, and they left.

Joy was both relieved and sick with apprehension. Her enjoyment in this evening was fully gone, but she wasn't ready to face the censure she was certain was coming.

The drive home was completed in ominous silence, making her stomach churn.

The second they walked into the penthouse, she blurted, "I'm so sorry."

"*You* are. Why?" Axel asked with muted outrage. "I

knew where you worked when we married, Joy. There's no reason for you to be sorry. God." He poured drinks for both of them, asking sharply, "Have you told anyone?"

"*No.* Only Heskel's friend, Zander, the dance instructor he took me to that one time, but Heskel asked him to keep it confidential." Would Axel balk at her pursuing dance now, worried it would inflame the rumors?

"This stinks of Otto." Axel brought her a glass and took a deep gulp from his own. "The next time you speak to your father, ask if anyone has been snooping around."

"He knows not to talk to reporters." Axel had warned her their marriage would generate curiosity. "But the neighbor knew," she recalled.

"He must have had someone investigate you, looking for something to undermine our marriage. He's trying to damage my reputation when I'm on the verge of competing with him. He's trying to—" He bit that off and looked away, profile flexing with remorse.

"What?" she prompted, sensing something unpleasant was coming.

His mouth tightened, before he said reluctantly, "He's trying to build a case for not accepting you as his daughter."

For rejecting her.

Against her will, a low sob resounded in her throat, leaving an ache in her chest.

"I shouldn't have said that," he said.

"Why not? It's true." Her throat hurt. She had been fully prepared for *Axel* to reject her over this, but he seemed to be infuriated on her behalf. "What are you going to do?"

"Everything in my power to destroy him," he said with a curl of his lip and another sip of his drink.

"I mean about how this ruins your reputation."

"I didn't say it ruins it. I said he's trying to damage it. If he wants to play dirty, I'd like to issue a press release that he's your father and sought you out for a marriage contract he refuses to honor. But that affects you and your family." He emptied his glass and set it down hard. "So I'll find another way to gut him."

He took the glass she offered that she hadn't touched.

"Can I..." She cleared her throat. "Can I talk to Dad first? To explain all of this so he's not blindsided by it?"

Axel's brows crashed together. "You would consider making a statement? You don't have to acknowledge that Otto is your father, Joy. He's caused you enough pain. Tonight—" He closed his fist and stalked a few steps away, shoulders a hard line. "I'm sorry. That should never have happened. The fact that you knew how to deal with that bastard's remark because you've faced derision like that before? You wouldn't have had to work in the club if Otto had reached out to you when he learned about you."

"I don't care about that." Her voice broke a little at how ferociously he was defending her. "It's not about money that he did or didn't promise me. I don't care about getting one up on him, either. I just don't want him to have the power to ambush me like that. If all of my secrets are out, and Dad knows about him, Otto can't use any of it against me. He ceases to have any power over me."

Axel set aside the glass and came to her. He settled one

hand on her hip, the other alongside her neck. His brow was pulled with concern, his gaze shadowed by remorse.

"I know I should apologize for drawing you into this, Joy, but Otto was always going to come after you. If not to keep me, to push out Mira. I'm sorry for what you're going through, but I'm not sorry for getting to you first and making this hard for him."

Her lips quivered. She had to press them together to steady them before she could speak.

"I thought you'd be angry at me. And think I was a liability." *I thought you'd send me home.* "I don't know what I bring to this marriage except—"

"You," he said, shifting his hand so he could set his thumb against her lips. "You bring you. That's enough."

Oh. Now she really was going to cry.

CHAPTER TWELVE

Joy's father took the news really well.

"I thought there was more to this marriage than you were letting on," Paul said in his creaky voice. "Your mother and I always expected you to be curious about your birth parents, sweetheart. You didn't have to hide this from me. I completely understand."

That made her feel weepy enough to want to hug him through the screen, especially when she confessed her meeting with Otto had not gone as well as she'd hoped.

After some consoling words, Paul said, "What about your husband? Please tell me you're still happy with your marriage?"

"I am." She blinked with shock at how true that was. Her life here with Axel was more fulfilling than she could have anticipated.

She went on to describe the dance company and the performance she was hoping to be picked for, the language classes she had signed up for and her upcoming getaway to Sicily with Axel, for business and sunshine.

A friendly journalist came by the next afternoon, bringing a photographer who took candid photos of her and Axel lounging around the penthouse and standing at the rail of the terrace. Joy wore off-white trousers with a torso-hugging, long-sleeved lace top in the same color. Axel wore a black suit with a black shirt and a black tie.

"You make a striking couple," the journalist said. "How did you meet?"

Joy let Axel take the lead. He was using this opportunity to announce he'd fully broken away from Otto and had opened a competing firm, confirming what was already floating through the headlines.

When Axel casually mentioned he had met Joy after learning she was Otto's daughter, the woman's eyes popped in realization she was being given a scoop.

"I only learned my birth father's identity very recently." Joy didn't mention Lorena's name but filled in a few blanks about her adoption into her American family, adding that she had wanted to meet Otto, but that they didn't have a meaningful relationship.

"Is my research correct? Were you performing as an exotic dancer prior to your marriage?" The journalist was giving Joy a chance to deny it.

"I was."

"Plug the company you're with now," Axel prompted her.

"I'm still in the audition process," Joy demurred. "But Axel is right. The choreographer deserves a mention for the production she's putting together." Joy offered up the dates and venue for the expected performance.

"Does your marriage have anything to do with you leaving Vorstoben?" the woman asked Axel. "By that, I mean the timing of your broken engagement to Mira Braun? She left the company, too. There seems to be some conflict between her and her father?" she probed.

"I can't speak for Mira," Axel said firmly. "Otto was aware for years that my plan was to run my own firm. I would prefer we hadn't come to legal action, but I'm confident the courts will side with me in our dispute."

The article came out the next day while they were on the ground in Sicily.

A small media storm ensued, but Axel was busy closing a deal on a massive resort complex that had ground to a halt due to various issues. That evening, they attended a mixer of executives and their spouses, and even though people seemed aware of the article and Joy's former job, everyone was more excited that their project had been saved than interested in gossiping about her.

When they returned to Berlin, Joy felt lighter than she had in years. Her family was thriving and looking forward to being together in California. Her financial troubles were gone. She no longer felt she had to hide her work at Martini's, and she was making new friends among her fellow dancers while doing what she loved.

The only thing she loved more than dancing every day was coming home to her husband.

They had fallen into a routine of discussing their plans for the day in the hot tub, parting after breakfast, then coming together again in the evening. Often, they went out again because they had engagements, but Joy was no longer afraid of those. She was seeing familiar faces and had been invited onto a charity board for performing arts that interested her.

She was on top of the world and told her brother that when he called one evening.

"I'm still trying to get used to this," David said with

concern. "It doesn't feel like *you*, Joy. I thought you wanted to be a nurse? What if you need something to fall back on?"

A wave of exasperated affection washed over her. David was caring and protective, but he didn't have a clue who she was at heart. Not the way Axel understood her.

"I'm dancing. I'm happy," she insisted. "You'll see when we come to California."

That trip was another month away, but she was looking forward to it. She and Axel would touch down in Chicago long enough to collect Paul before flying him to California themselves so Joy could help him get settled in his new home while meeting Carrie and David's newest addition.

"How's your brother?" Axel asked idly when they were undressing for bed.

"Good, but he asked me why I gave up the nurse training. You knew the day you met me that I was only pursuing it for Dad. That it wasn't my real passion. David was genuinely baffled that I would walk away from what he views as a solid profession. It made me realize how different I am from him. From all of them. They love me. I know that. And I love them, but I always felt this sense of being a bit of an oddity. Even my mother was very practical, working at City Hall because they had a decent pension. She encouraged my dance as a hobby while I was growing up, but it wasn't something she thought I should pursue as a living. They were concerned that I chose performing arts at college. When I gave it up for Todd, I think they were a little relieved. No one asked how I really felt about it."

"That's probably why you did give it up. You were trying to fit into their expectations."

"I really was," she said with dawning understanding. "I always had this lingering fear they'd reject me if I didn't stay between the lines. On the surface, Todd was cookie-cutter husband material. That's why I tried so hard to make it work with him."

"And when you realized he wouldn't make you happy, that their way didn't make *you* happy, you took up dancing for money, trying to show them that you could support them on your own terms."

"I wasn't that passive-aggressive about it. Not consciously, anyway." But he wasn't wrong. "I was trying to keep my dream alive in whatever way I could make it happen."

"Then I played on that to force this marriage on you, but I don't regret it. Not as much as I should." He took her hands and pulled them behind his back so she came up against him. "I see how much it means to you. It's where you feel you truly belong, isn't it?"

She nodded, growing emotional because he saw her so much more clearly than her family ever had.

I love him, she thought as she tightened her arms around him.

As his arms enfolded her, she knew she would remember this as the moment she fell. It wasn't even a fall. It was a sense of coming to rest. Because Axel might be demanding and remote and ferocious, but he always took such care with her.

His hands moved over her, and as so often happened with him, she felt pulled into him as though magnetized.

This was where belonged, she thought, closing her eyes against the press of heat behind them.

She tilted back her head, and they kissed, long and slow and with such a deep tenderness, her heart ached in the best possible way.

His hands moved lazily over her. They were still capable of frantic lovemaking, but neither of them was in a hurry tonight. This was a coming together that went beyond their bodies. For whatever reason, he was making her feel cherished, and she was drinking it up, wanting to give him all of herself. Not just her body, but the heart that felt cradled by his palm when he cupped her breast. The soul that condensed on the air when she gasped in pleasure.

I love you, she thought, as she licked beneath his ear and breathed his name toward the ceiling.

When she reached between them to caress his erection, he swore and said with quiet urgency, "I need to be inside you."

His hands went under her butt, and she hopped, grasping her arms around his neck and her legs around his waist. As he carried her to the bed and came down on her, she felt his erection against the tender folds that were aching to envelop him.

"You're shaking," he said.

"I want you so much," she said helplessly, feeling hot and wet and so aroused, she thought she would combust. "I don't know how to…" Express it. Reveal it. Make him feel it.

"Me, too."

Then they were tumbling across the bed, stripping off clothes until finally he pressed inside her.

They both calmed. Now his kiss turned languorous. He shifted so his weight was on one elbow, and he could send tingling pleasure through her with the lazy stroke of his hand. His knee crooked, and he secured their hips tighter, so they were locked like one of those brain-teaser puzzles she had never figured out how to unravel.

Who would want to? This was how they were meant to be. It was where she wanted to be. *This is home.*

I love you, she thought as he shifted over her and began to move in slow, powerful thrusts. *I love you*, she thought as the glorious tension built and sunlight filled her veins. *I love you*, was the only thought in her mind as the pleasure coalesced into a pinpoint of utter perfection, then expanding in waves of ecstasy.

His hand clamped on her shoulder, and his sweating body shook. A broken shout left him, and she lifted her hips for his final, rocking thrusts.

It was seismic. Cataclysmic. For a long, timeless moment, they were melded into one, caught in pure, shared ecstasy.

Joy wanted to stay in this liminal space of blissful unity forever, but physical reality crept in. Their hearts were pounding, their skin tacky enough to sting as he made the monumental effort to roll off her. Her body was weak, her mouth dry from panting.

But she was still in the glorious and dazed state of harmony. The words left her before she'd thought them through.

"I love you."

CHAPTER THIRTEEN

AXEL WAS ON his back, scraped clean of thought while his body was still recovering from lovemaking that had been intense even by the standard he and Joy usually set. His heart was still hammering, his chest billowing as his lungs snatched for oxygen.

She was on the pill now so he didn't have an excuse to roll away to remove the condom. He was too weak to do something like that anyway. And he couldn't do that to her. He might not know how to return that emotion, but if Joy was offering it to him, he couldn't reject it. Not when he knew how sensitive she was to being scorned.

But, *I love you*?

It shouldn't hurt like an acid burn, but it did.

"I didn't mean to say that," she whispered in an agonized voice.

"Did you mean it?" He turned his head on the pillow. "It's only been six weeks."

"I know." Her brow flinched, and her lashes dropped to hide her eyes. "I know that you…don't."

He looked to the ceiling, experiencing a new version of an old emotion: helplessness. He hated to hurt her and didn't know how to avoid it. It made him feel powerless—another emotion he couldn't bear.

His whole reason for marrying her had been to prevent Otto from taking advantage of him, but more frequently these days, he felt as though he'd taken advantage of Joy, building expectations in her that he couldn't fulfill.

"Joy—" He started to roll toward her, not sure what he would say, but she turned her back on him.

"I should get some sleep. Inga has already let a couple of dancers go. I want to be on my game tomorrow." She reached to turn out the light on her side.

He bit back a curse, aware he'd handled this badly but unsure how to fix it.

Things remained stilted between them. Axel was frustrated and mentally likened it to the way a storm or other natural event might thwart a project. It couldn't be changed or undone. It could only be weathered.

His mechanical brain wanted to find the solution, though. Or a way to prevent something like this from happening in future.

He channeled all his brooding into his new company, AxSev Engineering.

One of the key differences between himself and Otto was that Otto was a businessman who had taken over his father's engineering firm. Axel was an engineer who had become a businessman. Otto had also been born into wealth. He'd had a cushion to fall back on, so he was more comfortable with risk.

Axel had always taken a more methodical approach to his life, carefully amassing his material wealth to lay a foundation to support his next level. He brought the same attitude to his new company. Each investor and employee and potential project was inspected for quality and durability, like a brick in a structure he wanted to last for a thousand years.

Which wasn't to say things weren't happening quickly. He'd been deliberating on this for years. He knew what he wanted and took profound satisfaction in tapping every brick into place.

He could have been doing this two years ago, of course, but his resentment toward Otto over the delay had lost much of its edge, worn away by something he hadn't expected: Joy.

How could he hate Otto for procrastinating and manipulating him into this marriage when he liked being married to her?

At least he had liked it, before this discord had arisen between them.

He wanted to smooth things over, but Joy wasn't *here*. Even before this, she had been spending a lot of time at the studio and the fitness center, swimming laps to improve her endurance in a way that wouldn't cause her stress injuries.

She was determined to achieve her goals, and he admired her for that, but recognized a small jealousy inside himself over how much of her time was monopolized by it. He didn't want to feel threatened by it, but he did—maybe because he suspected she was using it to avoid him. He'd hurt her by not returning her love, and she had withdrawn.

The weight of being loved was so damned crushing, though. One of his earliest memories was his father saying, *Your Mutti loves you. She's counting on you to look after her when I'm not here.* Then his father had disappeared for a few weeks—serving time, Axel learned much later. What little money had been in his mother's purse had disappeared quickly, leaving Axel to scrounge food from a dumpster behind the grocer.

After his father died, his mother had said similar things countless times. *You're a good boy for taking care of me. I love you.* But those words had never put food on the table. Even when she'd finally embraced sobriety, her love had only felt like something that imposed a certain duty on him. *I know I was not the best mother to you, but I love you. I hope you'll forgive me.*

Axel was doing Joy a favor by not putting that sort of indebtedness on her. He met all her real needs, didn't he? He was giving her a very good life. Wasn't he?

He entered the penthouse to hear her upstairs, talking to someone. Her sister-in-law, it sounded like, judging by the excited babble of a toddler and the gurgle of laughter in Joy's tone.

"Okay, go show Abuela so I can talk with Tía," Carrie was saying as Axel reached the top of the stairs. "He misses you as much as I do, but get back to your text. She wants you as the lead?"

"One of them, yes. I'm very excited."

"That's fantastic! Congratulations! How are you going to celebrate?"

"Oh, I don't know," Joy said in a downplaying tone. "We have a party to go to this evening. I don't know the hosts, but these things are important to Axel, so I'll probably just buy myself a new leotard tomorrow. As if I need more of those!" She chuckled at herself.

"You deserve more than that," her sister-in-law chided. "This is a big deal. We'll do something big when you're here. We'll have a lot to celebrate by then."

"We will—Oh. Axel's home." Joy noticed him. The glow in her eyes dimmed to wariness, and her tone changed to the aloof one he was beginning to despise. "What time is the party?" she asked him. "I can be ready in twenty."

She wore her bathrobe. Her hair was pulled back from her freshly washed face, and she was midway through applying makeup.

"We have lots of time. Finish your call. Hello, Carrie." He stepped into view of the screen.

"Hi, Axel. It's good to see you, but I'll let you go," the very pregnant Carrie said. "I have to get ready for work. I was just excited when I saw Joy's text and wanted to congratulate her. Buy your wife some flowers," she instructed. "I'll talk to you both soon."

The women blew kisses at each other, and Joy ended the call.

"You got in?" Axel asked. "For the performance?"

"I did." A little of the sparkle returned to her eyes, and she couldn't seem to fight the grin that pulled at her lips as she added with shy pride, "As one of the leads."

"Why didn't you call me?" The fact she seemed to have texted her family without telling him was a surprisingly deep cut.

"I was going to tell you when I saw you." She sounded defensive and turned back to her makeup and the mirror.

"Well, I'm proud of you." He drew her back around and into a hug, even picked her up.

She stiffened in surprise as he turned in a circle and set her back on her feet, then she released a soft laugh of surprise, flustered and blushing. "Thank you." Her expression shifted into earnestness. "I couldn't have done it without you so, really. Thank you."

"Don't say that." He knew what dance meant to her. He was glad that he had some tiny part in making this happen for her, but he squeezed her shoulders and rubbed the soft velour of the robe down her arms. "You did the work to earn it."

"I know, but..." She shrugged, then shifted away from his touch.

He simply couldn't stand it any longer. "Carrie is right. We should celebrate. Let's skip the party and spend the weekend in Heiligendamm. The days are warm enough for beachcombing. It won't be overrun with tourists yet."

She lifted her gaze, properly meeting his eyes for the first time in days while her brow quirked with tentative optimism. "Really?"

If it meant she would quit avoiding him? "Yes."

They left within the hour, taking a helicopter to an elegant resort on the Baltic Sea.

Joy had been wallowing in misery for days. She had been okay with being in a loveless marriage before she'd fallen in love herself. Before she'd *said* it.

Maybe, if she hadn't had a bone-deep legacy of being rejected, she could have withstood Axel's rebuff more easily, but she kept wondering whether she was actually lovable. Yes, her family loved her, but they didn't fully understand her. The man who did understand her didn't love her.

The one thing that had saved her this week was dance. It had given her an outlet for her sorrow and loneliness and yearning and unrequited feelings. Inga had hugged her when she offered her the lead, calling her "one of our brightest stars."

In the dance studio, at least, she was truly wanted. Integral, even.

She wasn't sure if Axel was trying to spoil her to make up for their fight—which hadn't even been a fight. She was glad to spend time with him. She loved him. Of course she wanted to be with him, but she also felt as though she walked around without a layer of skin, everything feeling raw and exposed.

She was instantly charmed by the historic buildings, though, all painted white. He had booked them into a tower suite of a luxury hotel, one with two floors and endless views of the water. She couldn't help but relax as they strolled the beach before dinner, then wilted themselves in the sauna. The next day, they had a couple's massage, walked, ate delicious food and made love.

It was good. It always was. She felt as though her soul was wrenched from her body, but when it was over, she couldn't relax in his arms the way she used to do. She made an excuse to use the bathroom, then asked, "Do you mind if I catch up on my sleep?"

He seemed surprised but rose to make a few calls.

This should have been the reconnection they needed, but she couldn't help keeping a certain guard up, even as she called herself a fool for letting his reaction to her confession bother her so much. He cared about her. She knew he did. He gave her a good life. And he was right. They hadn't been together very long.

She tried to let go of her hurt and simply enjoy their time together.

On Sunday, she brought their refilled coffee mugs up to the bedroom and sighed at the glorious view of sunshine and dark blue water. "I could look at that forever."

"Do you want to stay another night?" Axel set aside his phone.

He was on the bench seat that ran under the line of windows facing the sea. He slouched against pillows piled into the corner and rearranged himself, waving to invite her to join him.

She sat in front of him so her back was against his chest, tailbone in the V of his opened legs. Sunshine poured over them, and a fresh, salty breeze came in through the open windows.

"I would love that, but I can't," she said, trying to relax into his warmth. "I probably won't even have a full weekend free until after the show. We have costume fittings coming up and meetings about set design."

He made a grumbled noise of dismay and draped his forearm across the front of her shoulders.

"I will try not to be impatient while your dancing takes you away from me. I am very proud of you, you know. In fact..." His long arm stretched behind her, to a nearby table, then came back with a velvet box the size of a deck of cards.

"What—? Axel, that's not necessary." A pang hit her heart as she looked at the box. It was a glancing blow, the kind that was an elbow in the face, unintentional, but it still hurt like hell.

"To commemorate your achievement." He opened it to reveal a gold chain of intricate links and a pretty pendant. A freeform pearl was trapped inside a cage of gold where the swirling bars were encrusted with tiny diamonds.

It was beautiful, but... She swallowed.

"You don't like it?" he asked into the silence.

"I—I'll wear it if you want me to." Her voice cracked as she heard how ungrateful she sounded. "I don't want *things* from you, Axel." She sat up and moved down the bench, instantly chilled.

"I don't know what else to give you, Joy. Things are all I have," he said darkly. He turned on the bench so his own feet hit the floor. He snapped the case closed and dropped it in the yawning space between them. "At least you can sell this if—"

"If what?" she asked with alarm.

"I don't know. If you're hungry and don't have anything else."

She saw then how deeply his early years of poverty still affected him. This was why he didn't trust, why he couldn't offer all of himself. "I would never sell a gift from my husband."

"Apparently, you're not even going to accept it."

She stared into his affronted glare, heart aching, and thought, *You didn't want my love when I offered it*.

His phone rang.

He sent an annoyed glance over his shoulder to where he'd left it on the windowsill. They had turned their phones off yesterday, but apparently their second honeymoon was over. He reached to answer it.

Joy tucked her hands under her thighs, staring at the unmade bed with its pillow-top mattress and abundance of pillows and luxury linens.

Look what you have, she scolded herself for the millionth time. Did it really matter that he hadn't said those words back to her?

Or did it matter doubly because she was settling for less than she deserved again, afraid that if she pushed for what she really wanted, he would reject her and she'd have no one?

"Mira?" he said crisply into his phone.

Joy heard the muffled feminine tones, but couldn't hear what was said. She didn't have enough German to follow it anyway. The way Axel went very still, however, pulled her spine and shoulders tight.

He said a few things in a hollow tone, then ended with, "Bis später," which he said to Joy all the time when he was on his way home.

"What happened?" she asked, stomach pulled into knots of apprehension.

"Otto's housekeeper just called her. The police and coroner are on their way. Mira's going there now."

Not an ambulance. "He's gone?" Joy's mind couldn't even comprehend it.

"They suspect a heart event. It seems to have happened when he was on his way to bed last night." His voice was low and somber. "I said I'd inform Umberto and the board."

He was already bringing his phone to his ear, not giving her a chance to say anything. Not giving her a chance to console him.

Did he need consoling? She couldn't tell.

She rose to dress, thoughts as scattered as the belongings they'd littered about the room. They would have to leave as soon as possible. She began to shake out a shirt to fold it for packing.

"Wirklich?" Axel sounded as though the word was punched out of him.

She snapped her head, watching him as he exchanged a few more words, then ended the call.

She dropped the clothes in her hands and went across to him.

"What happened? Are you okay?" She instinctively set a hand on his shoulder. It was both slumped under a great weight and steely with tension.

"No. Yes. Fine," he lied as he rubbed his stubbled jaw. "I told Umberto we're on our way back." He stood and found the trousers and shirt he'd worn to dinner last night. "Mira said the housekeeper called her because she though Mira was his next-of-kin, but given all of this..." He waved between them. "Mira wasn't sure. That's why she called me."

An arrow seemed to spear into Joy's chest. She clutched at the pain there.

"*I'm* not," she protested. "Am I?"

"Umberto said there will have to be a will search, and the validity of Otto's marriage contract is still to be determined by the courts, but as far as he knows, Otto left Vorstoben to me."

CHAPTER FOURTEEN

Axel was in shock. How could he not be? Otto had been reaching retirement age, but he had seemed in good health. This was the last thing Axel had expected to happen.

Which prompted the chilling thought that he had killed Otto himself by taking such an aggressive stance and putting so much pressure on him.

He saw the same self-recrimination in Mira's drawn face when they came together in Umberto's office that afternoon. Umberto was freshly shaved, but his hair was rumpled and his tie looked as though he'd already given it a yank from his throat.

It was only the three of them there, all in somber suits behind a closed door while rain buffeted the window.

"This will was in place before Otto learned of Joy's existence. Forgive me for being blunt," Umberto said to Mira, "but Otto took the attitude that if he was leaving the company to someone who was not his biological child, he preferred it go to Axel."

"That's not news," Mira said in a strained voice.

"In terms of his other assets, most were acquired during his marriage to your mother and are considered joint property, so he agreed you were entitled to those. We had been discussing other options since he had learned he had a biological child. He had intentions around leaving something to Joy, but as his marriage contract demonstrated, he wanted her to live here and have a firm connection to his life before he made any changes to these arrangements. That's why he stipulated you should be married to her for a year before he would transfer the shares." He turned to Axel now. "At this point, your wife stands to inherit nothing. There is room to challenge that with the marriage contract, if you wish to pursue it."

Did Axel want to enforce the contract and incite more bad blood with Mira so his wife could have a piece of the pie?

"It would muddy things and take time for the courts to make a decision," Umberto warned. "I expect that would have further negative effect on the company." The lawyer was nudging them toward accepting Otto's wishes as they were currently stated.

"I'll discuss it with Joy." Axel rubbed his jaw, still unable to fully take this in. He walked out with Mira a few minutes later, both of them silent until they were in the elevator.

"Drink?" Axel suggested.

"God, yes," Mira breathed.

They walked across the street to the bar in a hotel lobby. It was quiet, being midweek and the hour between the lunch and dinner rush. They ordered, then sat in silence.

"I should have reached out to you sooner. It's been…" How did he describe these last weeks of a whirlwind marriage and breaking away from a man who, it turned out, had wanted him to have the company he'd been fighting to take? "How have you been? Are you and DeStefano—"

"No," she cut in with a strained look on her face.

Axel dropped it. He had warned Mira off Rocco years ago, aware that Otto had a grudge against the man. He still didn't know what that was about, but Mira seemed to have decided Otto's rival wasn't her best ally after all.

She nodded a thank-you as their drinks were delivered and took a deep sip from hers.

"When I spoke to the head of the board, he asked what terms I'd set to come back as CEO," Axel said. The board didn't know yet that Axel was in line to inherit Otto's majority share, but he knew for a fact they'd been at panic stations from the moment Axel had left on his honeymoon. Things had been falling apart ever since, growing worse as Mira had gutted the financial ledgers.

"I had a call from him, too," she said. "They assumed I would be inheriting Otto's shares and wanted to know if I'd support you as CEO or if I would insist on running the company myself."

"What did you say?"

"I wanted to tell them the truth. All of it," she said with embittered weariness. "But I said something noncommittal because I've already done enough damage to Vorstoben. None of this is your fault. Or theirs. The company didn't do this to me. He did. My mother did." Tears of betrayal came into her eyes, but she blinked them away, chin coming up, gaze pointing out the window.

"You're entitled to an executive position, Mira. You've put in the hours. Otto never gave you enough credit or let you shine to your full potential. Tell me what you want."

"I don't even know anymore," she said with a strain in her voice. "I thought I did, for about a minute." She threw him an ironic smile. "It's so true to form that he didn't even give me the fight I wanted." Her gaze turned agonize, but curious. "What's she like?"

"Takes after her mother, one presumes, since she has a big heart." He was being facetious but also sincere. "She dances. Beautifully. She's very passionate about it. She's funny. Gutsy when she needs to be." He was saying too much and set his teeth together.

"You sound like you like her a lot. Did he?" Mira asked with a scathing edge on her tone.

"No," Axel said flatly. "He was furious that I married her without telling him. He took it out on her. I never should have brought her here. It was cruel."

"You mean he was."

Not just Otto. All Axel had wanted was this company, certain Joy's participation in their marriage could be bought for the right price.

I don't want things from you.

She had wanted more than assets from Otto, too. Acceptance. Welcome. Love.

"I knew how he would behave and I brought her here anyway." Like a lamb to the slaughter. He had hoped that she was confusing lovemaking and love again, but guilt was rising in him like a tide. She loved him, and he was hurting her as badly as Otto had.

All of this for something he was going to get anyway.

I helped her, though. She's dancing again. Surely that counted for something?

"I think his death is my fault," Mira whispered, face

crumpling with repentance. "I knew he was taking blood thinners. When I saw you'd married her, I knew he would be angry about it. I sent him flowers congratulating him on his daughter's marriage. Vile, right?"

"Don't do that to yourself." Before learning compassion from his wife, it wouldn't have occurred to Axel to stand and draw Mira into a hug, but he couldn't let her wallow in blame.

"I—" She was startled. They'd never been affectionate with each other, but she let him hug her and briefly rested her head on his chest. He heard her take a shaken breath.

"I did my share of pulling his supports," Axel acknowledged. "I publicly shamed him. Let's remember that he was reaping what he sowed."

"I suppose." She drew back, mouth pouted with sadness, and patted his lapel. "Thank you. I… Can I just say…" She lifted a crooked smile to him. "Our marriage never would have worked. This feels like I'm hugging my brother."

"Agreed," he said wryly and cupped her shoulder so he could set a very brotherly kiss on her brow. "We'll see a lot of each other over the next few days, but call me anytime."

"I will. And don't feel guilty about getting the company, Axel. You put in the time, too. I've always known you were the best person to run it."

Axel didn't come home until well after the dinner hour. He had a five o'clock shadow and his tie was over his arm with his jacket. His shirt sleeves were rolled up, his shirt open at the throat. He looked exhausted. He went straight to the sideboard to pour a drink.

"I've been in meetings with Gerard and some people with Vorstoben, getting out a press release." He sighed wearily. "Otto has some distant cousins, but the funeral arrangements seem to have fallen onto Mira and me. We agree that it's best to hold a service as soon as possible."

"Is there anything I can do?" Joy felt sick every time she thought about the fact she'd only met Otto once. Now her birth father was gone, and she would never have another chance at a relationship with him. Not that she was sure she would have wanted one, but it felt so final to know she never could.

"Heskel is taking lead with one of Otto's assistants." Axel threw back his drink in one go, then hissed out a breath. "Umberto said Otto's most recent will leaves the company to me. Everything else was joint property with Mira's mother, so it's going to her. If we accept this will, I can start pulling Vorstoben out of its nosedive immediately. Every day counts at this point. But you have the option of suing for what Otto promised to you in the marriage contract." He turned to face her.

She blinked. Then released a husky chuckle that held no humor. "Wouldn't that mean using your money to sue you for half of a company that you would run anyway? And wouldn't I have to wait until we completed our year of marriage?"

"Yes. But you said this was never about the money," he reminded her in a challenging tone.

"It's not." She tried not to be insulted by his assertive tone, remembering he was still processing all of this himself, but she still felt superfluous. Pushed away. "I've never felt I had a right to things that Mira believed were hers," she added in a murmur.

"Good. I need to make some calls." He walked into his office and closed the door.

That was it? Decision made?

She stood there for a few minutes, wondering if she had made a huge mistake in letting go of her option to sue. Her reasons for marrying Axel had never been about getting anything from Otto, but Axel had made certain promises to convince her to marry him.

Her own words echoed in her ears.

Wouldn't I have to wait until we completed our year of marriage?

Biting her thumbnail, she sent a message to her lawyer, then fell into bed. It had been a long day, and her mornings started early now, so she could get her stretches in before heading to the studio.

She didn't speak to Axel until breakfast the next day.

"I need my driver," he told her. "Heskel is arranging one to get you back and forth to the studio. Discuss it with him if you have any issues."

She almost demurred, but she could see he had a lot on his mind. At least, that was what she hoped was behind his terse, distracted tone.

She couldn't escape the thought that Axel didn't need to be married to her anymore. He had only proposed to get Vorstoben, and now he had it. Did he even want to be married to her anymore?

The next few days passed in a blur. LaShonda said she would review the prenup contract and get back to her. Joy then missed an afternoon dance rehearsal to attend Otto's service.

She wasn't sure if it was the somber nature of the afternoon or all that was going on, but she felt very removed from Axel even when she stood beside him. They had barely seen each other since being away. They shared the bed for a few hours every night, but they hadn't made love.

At the service, most of the people were from Vorstoben. Joy didn't know any of them, but she smiled when she caught up with Heskel's husband, Klaus. They'd only met a few times, and she was a little surprised he was here, considering he'd been treated so badly by Otto when he had his accident.

Klaus grinned wryly, saying, "Technically, I've been rehired by Vorstoben. Axel is keeping AxSev as an ancillary division. I'll be the head engineer there. You didn't know?"

It was another example of how estranged they'd become in a few short days.

"He's been so busy, we've barely spoken," she murmured, then saw Axel was looking for her. "Excuse me." She hurried over to him.

"You two haven't met. Mira, Joy." Axel introduced her to the tall brunette.

Mira wore a black dress that flattered her slender frame. She spoke through the dotted veil on her tiny black hat. "It's nice to meet you."

"And you," Joy said sincerely, holding out her hand. "I'm very sorry…" Her voice trailed off. Was she sorry for Mira's loss? Sorry her birth mother had had an affair with a man who was married to Mira's mother? "I'm sorry this is such a complicated mess," she said with a pained smile.

"Me, too." Mira's lips twisted with pained humor. "I'll also preemptively apologize for stealing so much of your husband's time in the next while. There's a lot to be dealt with, and I don't really have anyone else to lean on." Mira flinched as she said that.

Joy had the impression the anguish in her expression had nothing to do with losing Otto. She almost suggested they have a glass of wine sometime, but the service started.

It was yet another long, draining day. When they got home, Axel said, "Hot tub?"

"I have an early morning. I need to sleep." She could have stayed up with him. The hot tub often led to lovemaking, and she could have used that stress release and a feeling of closeness with him.

Except she wasn't sure how close they were anymore. She kept thinking, *He doesn't need me.* It left an ache in her chest that she avoided by diving into sleep.

They didn't have a proper discussion until two days later, on Saturday. She was dozing when Axel reached across the mattress for her.

"You're here," he said with sleepy discovery, grazing his palm over her hip, then pulling her closer.

Her blood zinged the way it always did when she came into contact with him, but she stiffened, panicking that she would turn emotional—desperate, even—if she made love with him.

"I thought you had the day off," he said as she rolled away and sat up on the far edge of the bed.

"I do, but I have a costume fitting later."

"Joy." He sighed as he rolled onto his back. "We need to talk."

"I know." She didn't want to, though. She would hear things that hurt. Maybe he might even say that he didn't want to be married to her any longer.

She stood and began to dress in yoga pants and a loose shirt.

"Are you angry about the contract? That I said you shouldn't pursue it?" He stayed in the bed propped on an elbow, looking dangerously sexy with his shadowed jaw and heavy eyelids.

"I'm the one who said I didn't want to pursue it." She ran a brush through her hair, then twisted it into a clip.

"What then? You're still upset that…"

She turned to stare at him.

His jaw was clenched, his mouth tight, his gaze flinty.

"You're not going to say it?" she asked on a bitter laugh. "Yes, I am still upset that you don't love me."

"Joy." He flinched.

"I know that's not something you can control. I don't blame you for it." Her voice broke. "I just can't help thinking there's a reason you can't love me. That I lack something—"

"Don't." He threw off the covers and stood, then yanked on his underwear. "The flaw is in me. I don't know how to give you what you need."

"Then why keep me here?" The words blurted out of her.

He paused closing the fly on his jeans to stare at her. "Is there somewhere you'd rather be?" His tone was very deep and ominous.

"I'm asking what you gain if I stay." Her heart was in her throat, thinning her voice to a strident pitch while her lips stuttered out the questions that had been plaguing her. "What do you need me for now that you've got Vorstoben? You don't need to shove me down Otto's throat. You don't need to prove to anyone that this is a real marriage. I don't know how much longer I can keep pretending it is."

His head snapped back. "It's as real as it's likely to get."

"Yes, I know that." That was why she had completely lost faith in it.

His zip was overly loud as he yanked it closed. "So you want to leave?"

"I can't, can I?" Silently, she ordered herself to shut up. She was ruining everything, but her mouth kept going. "I can't leave you unless you release me. That's what LaShonda said. If I walk away, I lose all the support for my father. That's what I get from this marriage, but what do you get? Orgasms? Was I supposed to give you one of those this morning?"

"Those are voluntary, and I was under the impression you liked them as much as I do. But if you want my permission to leave, then you have it," he snapped. "Go. I release you."

She sucked in a breath, astonished by how easily he said it. By how much it hurt. He wasn't even going to try to fight for her? He really didn't want her.

Her phone alarm began to burble. She snatched it up to silence it, remembering why she'd set it. She scooped up her handbag from the table by the closet and started down the stairs.

"That's it? You're leaving?" His voice seemed to echo off the rafters. "That tells me exactly how much you love me, doesn't it?"

She stopped on the stairs and looked backward at him, unable to believe he'd said that.

He stood in the open doorway to their bedroom. His bedroom. His house. She'd never felt more like a houseguest in this marriage.

"I'm due for my costume fitting," she said with the last threads of her fraying poise.

It was a white lie. The alarm was to remind her to wake up in time. She didn't have to leave right now. She only wanted the excuse to leave, before she fully broke down in front of him.

"And you never even wanted my love," she reminded him. "So fine. I take it back. I release you."

"Frau Severin." The doorman looked up with a smile as she came out of the elevator. "This came for you this morning. I didn't want to call up too early—are you all right?"

"Fine," she lied and took the envelope he offered her, shoving it into her bag and walking outside. That was when she remembered her driver wasn't coming for another hour.

She started walking. She knew the route well enough by now that she covered the distance to the studio in steps of blind fury and acute heartache, arriving early for her fitting.

Thankfully, the appointments were staggered, so there were only a few people in the room when Joy walked in with swollen eyes and a face splotchy from crying.

"What happened?" Inga asked with startled concern.

"A spat with Axel." It was so much worse than a spat. *Go. I release you.*

Joy was devastated. Her instinct was to catch the first plane home, but as she stood for her fitting, she knew she couldn't let a man knock her off her stride again. Even if her marriage was over, her dance career wasn't. She would stay in Berlin at least until after the performance.

How, though? Where?

She was trying to figure things out as she picked up her bag. Her phone was pinging with texts, so she glanced at the screen. There were two from her driver and another from Axel.

Your driver is here. Where are you?

Where did he think? Gawd. She silenced her notifications and dropped her phone into her bag, noticing the envelope the doorman had given her.

She opened it, mostly to put off having to go home to face Axel again. Then she had to lean on the wall, finding herself on the floor by the time she had finished reading.

She started again, trying to take it in.

My dear,
I believe you are my niece. My sister was Lorena Fontaine. I'm in Berlin on business this week. My number is

below. I would very much like to meet you if you have time. I'm staying with my wife at—

"Joy?" One of her fellow dancers crouched down before her, asking with concern, "Are you okay?"

"What?" She touched the tickle on her cheek and realized she was crying again, this time for a whole new reason. "Yes." She was better than she'd been in a very long while. "Do you have a car? I need to go to a hotel."

CHAPTER FIFTEEN

AXEL WOULD NEVER have described himself as someone who snapped, but this morning that was exactly what had happened. He'd been trying to hold on to Joy since she had confessed her love, but she'd been slipping away from him, bit by bit.

I don't want things from you. Why keep me here? I don't know how much longer I can keep pretending.

There'd been such rejection and stark unhappiness in her words he'd arrived at his breaking point. There had always been an expiry date on their relationship. She was right. He didn't need her. Not the way he had two months ago when he proposed to her.

Even so, he'd been blindsided by the fact she felt trapped and wanted to leave him. When she had mapped out why she couldn't, a host of emotions had accosted him: guilt at holding onto her. Inadequacy that he wasn't offering enough. Anger that she was reducing their marriage to money and orgasms. Hurt.

Yes, he'd been hurt by the way she'd been shutting him out, so he'd snapped and told her to go. Then he'd been so stung as she walked away, he'd taken a shot that was fathoms beneath him.

She'd responded exactly as he deserved, by throwing his own words back in his face.

You never even wanted my love. So fine. I take it back. I release you.

She might as well have plunged a knife into his chest. Every breath hurt.

The buzz from the doorman yanked him from his brooding.

"Yes," he said curtly.

"Frau Severin's driver is here. I explained that she left an hour ago. She hasn't answered his texts. Did you have any instructions for him?"

"She *walked* to the studio?"

"I presume so?"

Axel tried texting her but didn't get a reply, so he sent the driver to the studio, expecting she would need a lift home.

A few minutes later, the driver informed him she wasn't there.

"Ask Inga to call me," he instructed the driver.

"She was here," the choreographer said when he answered her call. "But she left at least thirty minutes ago."

"Walking? Did she say she was coming home?" Axel asked.

"I didn't ask. Although…" She cleared her throat and lowered her voice. "She seemed upset when she arrived."

Yeah. He knew.

"Let me know if you hear from her," he said gruffly, thinking, *Please. Please let her be all right.*

Of course she was all right, he thought impatiently. It sounded like she had walked to the studio because she was angry with him. She was probably walking home, still clearing her head and cooling her temper. She had started to get her bearings in the city and knew which streets to avoid. She was picking up enough German to ask for help if she needed it. She was resourceful. She'd grown up in Chicago, for God's sake. She was tough enough to deal with anyone who got fresh with her.

None of that reassured him. A sick churn of gravel sat in the pit of his gut, urging him to hit the Undo button and take back those biting words he'd hurled at her. *Go. I release you.*

What the hell had possessed him?

Restless, he took a quick inventory to see if she'd taken anything more than her handbag. Her dance bag was here. Her passport was in the safe. Her jacket was in the closet.

She hadn't left him. Even though he'd told her to.

The ache in his chest sharpened. Where the hell had she gone?

When his phone rang, he snatched it up, but it was only Mira.

"Yes?" he said tersely.

"I have to get Otto's mansion ready for sale. It occurred to me, there's so much art there. I took what belonged to Mom ages ago, so everything there is something Otto bought. Joy should have a look and take what she wants. It's not family portraits or anything, but she should have something of his, even as an investment."

"I'll mention it when I see her. She's out."

"You sound mad. What's wrong?" she asked with concern.

"We had a fight. She went to the studio and should

be home by now, but she's not. And she's not answering my texts." *And it's all my fault.*

"Do you want to talk about it?"

"No."

"Is that the reason you're fighting?" she asked dryly.

"I told her to leave," he admitted. Saying it aloud closed an icy fist around his heart, squeezing it into the base of his throat. How could he be so stupid? So cruel?

"*Why?* You seemed to really care about her."

"I do," he said through his teeth. "But—" *I was afraid to care that much.* Love was sold as a profound source of strength, but in his experience, it was nothing but a sense of helplessness.

So he'd fought against succumbing to it. Yet here he was. Helpless.

"Axel." Her voice turned admonishing. "You said Otto was awful to her. I don't know what it's like to be adopted, but I do know what it's like to wonder why someone who is supposed to care about you doesn't. If you acted like you cared, then told her to leave—"

"I know," he said through his teeth, barely able to withstand the clench in his chest.

I just can't help thinking there's a reason you can't love me.

He had promised to protect her from Otto, then hurt her worse than anyone else ever had.

"I have to go. I need to find her."

Joy had texted Lowell Fontaine that she was coming to his hotel. He met her in the lobby along with his wife, Pascale.

Then he took Joy by the shoulders, and his eyes—eyes that were the same shape as her own—grew damp. "It's like she's here, still with me. You look just like her. I didn't know. I'm so sorry that I didn't know about you." He hugged her.

"Oh, chère," Pascale said. "Perhaps she doesn't want—"

"Je suis désolé." Lowell started to release her.

"No, it's okay," Joy chuckled weepily and hugged him back. Hard. She closed her eyes and drank up what she'd hoped Otto would offer her: instant, unconditional acceptance.

Somehow Pascale herded them into an elevator, and Joy soon found herself in the well-appointed lounge of a suite. Refreshments arrived, but she barely noticed.

"I didn't know if any of her family knew about me," she said. "It seemed like she didn't want anyone to know."

"This is true," Lowell said with regret. "It didn't even occur to me Lorena might have had a child, not until Pascale saw the notice about Otto's death. Frankly, my only thought on Otto's passing was 'good.' I'm sorry if you feel differently about him, but he treated Lorena abominably. She was young, thought herself in love. He dazzled her with gifts, but she was his mistress, so he was ashamed of her. I thought that was the worst of it, but when I learned he had made her give up her child?"

"He didn't know about me." Joy explained how Otto had come to find out. "How did you realize I was her daughter?"

"There was a photo of you and your husband with the article on Otto. Pascale pointed you out to me. She noticed how much you looked like Lorena."

"He brushed me off," Pascale said, taking over. "But reading that Otto was your birth father, I just knew. The timing fit. Lorena missed our wedding because she went to New York. She and I had a terrible falling out over it. She had introduced me to Lowell. She was supposed to be my maid of honor, but she was adamant about leaving. Now I realize she knew she would have been showing on our wedding day."

"Our parents cut her off when they learned of their affair," Lowell broke in sadly. "They wouldn't have helped her if she'd told them she was pregnant. I could have been kinder. She asked me for money to help her get to New York. I was glad she was leaving Otto, but I said she should wait until after the wedding. I don't know where she got the money. Sold some of the jewelry he'd given her, I suppose. It breaks my heart. If I'd been more willing to help her, she might have kept you."

"When she came back, things were still strained between us," Pascale said with equal regret. "I didn't want to forgive her. It seems so childish now, to hold a grudge over something so inconsequential. She must have been so frightened. Heartbroken. She was different when she came home. Older. Quieter."

"But she went back to him?" Joy recalled.

"She did. I never fully understood what she saw in him. He was very rich, obviously. And very handsome," Pascale admitted reluctantly. "Their second affair didn't last long. She told me she thought he was ready to leave his wife, but he wasn't. She said they'd both changed. That's when she moved to Heidelberg and opened the bookstore."

"Did she marry? Have more children?"

"No." There were bright tears in Pascale's eyes. "I always assumed Otto broke her heart. Now I'm sure that giving up her daughter did that."

"Oh." Joy covered her trembling mouth.

Pascale moved to sit next to her and rubbed her shoulders.

"We hope you'll meet our children, though?" Lowell said hesitantly.

"I have cousins?" Joy picked up her head.

"Two boys and a girl," he said with pride. "We haven't told them any of this. We wanted to meet you first and see if you were open to it?"

Fresh tears brimmed her eyes. "I would love that."

Axel went to the dance studio himself, catching Inga as she was leaving for the day.

"I still haven't heard from her," he told her, not mentioning that he could see Joy had her notifications silenced.

The choreographer hesitated, then sighed. "She told me you'd had an argument. I'm sure she's just taking some time for herself. Let me see if she's with any of my dancers." She texted a group chat. "Michael dropped her at a hotel a few hours ago."

She told him which one, and Axel went there, but when he asked the front desk to put him through to her room, she wasn't registered.

Had she met someone here? Who?

Axel ordered a drink in the bar, wondering what the hell he was going to do if she refused to come back to him. He had ignored a dozen calls today along with countless texts and emails, all to do with Vorstoben and projects that meant nothing to him. How could anything hold any meaning for him when the one person he cared about above all others was hurting and avoiding him?

The best case was that Joy was giving him the silent treatment because he'd hurt her. The worst case was that she was looking for somewhere to live because he'd broken her heart.

He had never wanted to feel this powerless, and the worst part was, he'd done it to himself. She wasn't doing this to him. She didn't think he cared about her, but he did. He cared so much it sat as a lump in his throat and was a hard stone lodged in his chest.

He loved her. That was what this agony was. He loved her, and he didn't know how he could push through the life he'd made for himself if he didn't have a reason to be in it.

His phone pinged.

He flipped it over, and his heart lurched when he saw it was finally a text from Joy.

On my way home. Will explain when I get there.

He threw a few bills onto the bar and walked out to the lobby in time to see her hurrying from the elevators toward the revolving doors. "Joy."

She jolted and turned, staring at him in shock as he crossed toward her. "What are you doing here?" she asked with astonishment.

"Looking for you." He looked to the elevator as though

he might catch a glimpse of whose room she was leaving. He had never felt so nauseous, so jealous, so terrified in his life. "Who were you with?"

"My uncle," she said with a bemused blink.

There was a taxi outside the hotel. They stepped into it, and Joy nervously relayed the story to Axel on their short drive home. He barely spoke, but he listened intently.

"They live in Lyon," she finished up as they entered the penthouse. "They have children. I have cousins."

"How did you get to the studio this morning? Did you walk? You didn't even take your jacket. Are you cold? Do you want to shower? Rest?"

"No, I'm fine."

"Hungry?"

"No, I had coffee and sandwiches with Lowell and Pascale." She dropped her bag onto the sofa, then lowered to the cushion beside it, blowing out a long breath. "I'm a little talked out, though."

"Good. Because I have a few things to say." Axel paced across her line of vision, then halted to glare at her. "Don't you *ever* worry me like that again."

He didn't raise his voice, but Joy jumped at his vehemence and pushed herself deeper into the sofa. "I didn't—"

"I'm not finished." His hand made a crocodile bite with fingers and thumb, telling her to shut her mouth.

Rude.

"I don't care how angry you are with me or how big of an ass I've been, you will text me proof of life when I ask for it."

"It was two hours—"

"Four and a half. You went to a hotel to meet strangers without telling me—"

"Are you being serious right now? This is an example of you being an ass, by the way. Should I text that to you?" She pretended to reach for her purse.

"I have been an ass since the day we met," he said angrily. "You had no business marrying me. And you claim to have had the bad judgment to fall in love with me. How can I possibly trust you to have any judgment where strangers in hotel rooms are concerned?"

"You're going to throw that in my face again?" She picked up the cushion from the corner of the sofa and hugged it, growing teary and stressed all over again. "I won't have that fight right now. I've had a really emotional day, Axel."

"I know what you're going to say."

"No, you don't!" She didn't let him cut in. "Because I don't. All I know is that I want to dance, and I promised Inga she could count on me. I know that 'show must go on' attitude sounds ridiculous or… I don't know how it sounds." She squeezed the cushion. "I only know that I can't let whatever happens between us cost me my chance to dance. Not again. So I'm staying in Berlin. I don't know what to tell you about whether I'm continuing this marriage or staying in this apartment because I'm really hurt."

"*You* are hurt," he scoffed, glaring at her with outrage, then shoving his hand through his hair. "Do you have any idea what has been going through my mind since the doorman told me your driver was here and you were long gone? You didn't even take a jacket."

That was the second time he'd mentioned that crime. She wasn't sure why he was so incensed about it. The April day had been quite pleasant.

"When I saw you'd turned off your notifications, I thought you were dancing. Maybe punishing me a little. Which I deserved, but I thought you would come home after you were done at the studio. You didn't take a jacket. You hadn't actually left me if all you had was your phone and a credit card."

Oh. She was starting to see why the lack of a coat was such a big deal.

"What other reason could there be then, when time wore on and you didn't come home? I was actually relieved to hear you had gone to a damned hotel with a male dancer because at least if you were having an affair, I knew you were alive."

"I wasn't having an affair."

"No, but if your aim was to show me how empty my life would be if you left me, mission accomplished."

"I've told you where I was. Are you really going to say I shouldn't have gone to meet my birth mother's brother?"

"No. But you didn't have to go alone. I would have gone with you if you'd asked. What does it say about where we're at that you didn't even think to call me and ask me to meet you there? You didn't trust me to be your support in that. Did you?" He ran his hand over his face, but not before she saw the anguish that flashed across his expression.

"I was just reacting," she murmured. "It felt urgent.

Like they would disappear if I didn't see them right away. I know that doesn't sound rational."

"I understand why you went, Joy. I do." He dropped his hand. "And I'm glad it went well, but what if it hadn't? What if it had turned out like it had with Otto, and you were rejected all over again, and I wasn't there to absorb some of that blow? You didn't even know that I wanted you *here*." He pointed at the floor. "For as long as we both manage to live."

Well, why did he have to say that? For someone who was being mostly an ass, he was also being sweet enough to make her blink back tears.

"I never should have told you to leave." His voice thickened with remorse. "It was stupid. Mean. I'm sorry I said it, and I hope you'll forgive me. But, Joy, I want you to be with me because you want to be with me. When you said you wanted to leave, I had to give you that. I don't know how to show how I feel except by giving you what you seem to need." He held out his open palms, helpless. "I feel a lot. I love you."

"Don't..." A knot formed behind her breastbone, but a tiny, tiny hope began to unfurl inside her. "Don't say that word if you don't mean it."

He came to sit on the coffee table and clasped her hands. He looked into her eyes, and there was such a fierce light there, her heart lurched toward hope, but she held it back, fearful.

"Refusing to say it doesn't make it not true," he said with disgruntlement.

"But you think love is something that makes you

weak. That hurts to carry. You don't want it." Her voice wavered.

"I said that," he acknowledged. "And it does hurt. It's a terrifying emotion, Schatz. It means that this…" He scanned his gaze all over her. "Any little harm to you might as well be a knife to my own heart. I can't stand when you're hurt. That's why I was so eaten up today when I didn't know where you were. I had hurt you, and I felt it so deeply. It was a self-inflicted wound, and I couldn't fix it because I couldn't find you. I love you," he repeated, hands tightening on hers.

She searched his face, very frightened she was dreaming and would wake up heartbroken all over again.

"I can see you're having trouble believing me. Look. The kind of love I grew up with was obligation and responsibility, but that's not what this is. I thought love was something that was imposed on you. Some entity I could choose to bring into our relationship or not. But it *is* our relationship. I realized that when you said you would take back your love. I knew you couldn't do that because I couldn't keep from loving you. I want to marry you again."

"What?"

He ran his thumbs across her knuckles and caught the pad of his thumb against her wedding rings. "I want to marry you for no reason except that we love each other. I want you in my life forever, Joy. We belong together. Do you think you would be willing to marry me again? For real this time?"

It wasn't just the words that made her vision blur with tears. It was the pledge. The emotion. The truth. The profound belief that settled over her that she really did have a place in his life, with him. Forever.

She had to bite her quivering lips as sweet love tumbled through her. She placed her hand against the side of his face, barely able to speak past the elation swelling her heart.

"I do."

EPILOGUE

Two years later...

JOY WAS TOO nervous to peek into the crowd before curtain, but Axel had sent her the requisite break-a-leg text, so she knew he was here. When the first notes of the score resounded through the small theater, she became completely focused on her cues and marks and delivering the best performance she could.

The techno-pop musical was loosely based on *The Threepenny Opera*. Mounting this production with fellow students had been part of her final grade, earning her a degree in performing arts. It had been so well received, they'd been able to persuade a local theater to give them a short run.

Singing was not Joy's natural talent, but she could match pitch in chorus numbers, and this production relied heavily on interpretive dance. In fact, she had choreographed some of the numbers, so she knew them through and through.

It was still nerve-racking, especially when she thought about doing this every night for—*No. Don't think about that now. Leap. Twirl. Exit stage left.*

She was sweating and panting at curtain call but exhilarated. The audience was on their feet, likely coaxed there by her family. Axel had bought out an entire row for Joy's family, flying them in for it. Even David was here, probably still trying to calm Carrie's nerves as she checked *one more time* with the professional nanny service minding their children at the hotel.

A short time later, still grinning with triumph, Joy joined everyone at a nearby hotel where her husband had arranged a champagne reception for the entire cast and their various guests. It was a late night for Paul, but he had been napping this afternoon when she left for the theater, and his newest medication seemed to be helping a lot with his symptoms. He and his new girlfriend, Nora, were chatting brightly with Lowell and Pascale.

Everyone was hugging her and gushing enough to make Joy blush.

"I was afraid it would be like one of those little kid plays with bad costumes and scenery falling over, but that was excellent," her cousin teased, winking at her.

Joy still couldn't get over having cousins. They had had a wildly different upbringing from hers, yet they felt so familiar to her, it was as though she'd known them all her life.

Quinn and Micah gave her a ridiculously enormous bouquet, and she received hugs and accolades from Inga, who was round with pregnancy, along with many more of her friends from the festival performance.

Heskel and Klaus were here and had even brought their friend Zander, the dancer who'd evaluated her two years ago. Zander kissed both her cheeks, complimented her performance *and* the choreography and said he would recommend the show to everyone he knew. Her knees almost unhinged.

It was so touching and overwhelming, Joy had a little cry later, once she and Axel were home and getting ready for bed.

"Honigbiene," Axel chided as he drew her into his arms. "What's this?"

"I'm just so happy." She slid her arms around his waist, hugging tight. "I never would have had this without you. Thank you."

"That is far more credit than I deserve. You were always going to find your way back to dancing, shining so brightly you steal every scene."

"I didn't."

"You did. I couldn't take my eyes off you."

"You're biased."

"Yes, but I'm also capable of seeing what's obvious." He brushed a tendril of hair behind her ear. "I won't be the least bit surprised if opportunities come to you after this."

"I hope so, but…" She quirked her mouth. "I want to dance, but I don't want to be away from you."

"Joy. You know I'll spend a year in New York if you want to audition for Broadway. We'll find a way to make it work. Do not let me hold you back."

"Thank you. But I do like our life here, and I wouldn't mind pursuing a master's degree. Also…" Was this the right time to bring it up?

His brows lifted.

"Well, you saw that Inga's expecting? She asked me if I would consider working with her on the festival production this year, since she'll be delivering in the middle of rehearsals. It got me thinking that maybe I could do that, too. Have a baby," she said tentatively. "We don't have to talk about it right now. I know you've always been ambivalent about children—"

He set the pad of his thumb over her lips. His expression was so tender, her heart hiccuped. "I used to think love was something I had to carry. That it wouldn't add to my life, but God, Joy, look at what your love has brought into my life. Everything is brighter. Better. Richer in ways I never would have understood if I wasn't married to you."

"Oh." Her eyes began to sting and well up.

"You think those little monsters of your brother's have no effect on me? Your nephew took my hand when we were crossing the road to come see your rehearsal, and I thought my heart would stop. The level of responsibility was terrifying, but so gratifying when I got him across safely."

She bit back her grin.

"You weren't here to see it, but your niece fell asleep on me the other day. I was annoyed that Carrie insisted on taking her to her cot. I thought, if we had our own, I could hold our sleeping baby as long as I wanted to."

Oh, this ridiculous man. "You really mean it? You want to start a family?"

"I want you to chase your career as long and hard as you need to, so I haven't said anything, but yes. I think about having children with you all the time. When you're ready, I will be ready. And, just to put it on the record, I'm open to adopting, if that's something you ever thought about."

Not a ridiculous man at all. One who was gifting her

the world, making her wonder how she had come to deserve it.

"Sometimes I wonder what my life would look like if you and I hadn't been forced together by Otto," she admitted somberly. "That scares me because I love you so much, I don't know where I would have put all of these feelings otherwise."

"Dance," he said simply. "And I would have seen you onstage somewhere and moved mountains to get to you."

Farfetched as it sounded, she believed him.

"Now, we don't have to try making a baby tonight, but maybe we should rehearse how it's done," he suggested.

Laughing, she leaped, and he caught her, then tumbled her onto the bed.

* * * * *

Did you fall head over heels for Business-Deal Bride*? Then be sure to check out the next installment in the Business Proposals duet, coming soon! And why not try these other stories from Dani Collins?*

His Highness's Hidden Heir
Maid to Marry
Hidden Heir, Italian Wife
The Greek's Wife Returns
Boss's Christmas Baby Acquisition

Available now!

(301)
908-0331